# "Pretend to
You've go

"Is the idea so abhorrent to you, Donna?"
Grant asked quietly. Please, will you do
it?"

"Do what exactly?" Donna hedged, unable
to ignore the plea in Grant's eyes. "It
would be easier if I knew how far you
expect me to go with this farce."

"Just let Carmen see that there's something
between us. It might be a casual embrace or
something more telling. I can assure you it
won't be so very unpleasant." Grant's tone
was surprisingly gentle.

"But there's something you're forgetting,"
Donna countered hastily, suddenly very
aware of this man's attractions. "Carmen
will hardly be fooled by any phony
embraces."

Grant smiled. "You're right, of course. We
could do with a little practice."

Practice! What had she got herself into?

**Miriam MacGregor** began writing under the tutelage of a renowned military historian, and produced articles and books—fiction and nonfiction—concerning New Zealand's pioneer days, as well as plays for a local drama club. In 1984 she received an award for her contribution to New Zealand's literary field. She now writes romance novels exclusively and derives great pleasure from offering readers escape from everyday life. She and her husband live on a sheep-and-cattle station near the small town of Waipawa.

## Books by Miriam MacGregor

HARLEQUIN ROMANCE

Don't miss any of our special offers. Write to us at the following address for information on our newest releases.

Harlequin Reader Service
901 Fuhrmann Blvd., P.O. Box 1397, Buffalo, NY 14240
Canadian address: P.O. Box 603,
Fort Erie, Ont. L2A 5X3

# *Autumn at Aubrey's*

## *Miriam MacGregor*

# *Harlequin Books*

TORONTO • NEW YORK • LONDON
AMSTERDAM • PARIS • SYDNEY • HAMBURG
STOCKHOLM • ATHENS • TOKYO • MILAN

Original hardcover edition published in 1987
by Mills & Boon Limited

ISBN 0-373-02890-3

Harlequin Romance first edition February 1988

# CHAPTER ONE

THE distant gleam of water told Donna she was approaching the trout-fishing mecca of Lake Taupo and, as the red Austin Mini topped a rise, she drove to the side of the road, stopped the car and gazed about her.

To the south and beyond the lake she could see the trio of snowclad volcanoes rising from the North Island's central plateau. Silhouetted against a pale cerulean sky, they reminded her of three sleeping giants, and it was a relief to know she did not have to drive as far as those mountains. Beryl had said that Aubrey's Place was situated only a few miles down the lakeside and, as the main highway skirted its twenty-five miles of length, the fishing lodge should not be too difficult to find. She slipped the car into gear and drove on.

A chilly westerly breeze swept in and blew strands of auburn hair across her cheek, causing her to wind up the window. As a child that same hair had been lighter and more Titian, earning her the names of Carrots, or Ginger but, now that she had reached the age of twenty-two, its colour had deepened to a reddish-brown. She had been more than thankful for the change.

Unchanged, however, were her dark-lashed hazel eyes with their tiny flecks of green and brown. Today they looked green, reflecting the warm woollen jersey that moulded her rounded breasts and slim waist. Below the green jersey her dark blue and green MacKay tartan trews emphasised her neat hips, while on the seat beside her lay a matching plaid jacket.

'Pack warm clothes,' Beryl had advised. 'It's April now, and that means autumn.'

Donna had obeyed, realising that the air of Taupo's

5

higher altitude would be much cooler than Auckland's sea-level atmosphere. And this became noticeable as she observed that frosts were already turning some of the trees to a variety of reds, ambers and yellows.

A short time later she drove through Taupo's wide main street which consisted of shops geared towards the tourist trade. It reached the lake, turned left and continued between the shore and the long stretch of waterfront houses. It passed a turn-off that would take travellers over the mountainous road to the east coast, then swerved right to follow the shore southward.

It can't be too far away now, she thought as the Mini sped over the miles of highway, and suddenly there it was—Aubrey's Place. Nor could there be any doubt, because large letters across the front proclaimed this fact.

Donna had not known what to expect of a fishing lodge, and she now pulled to the side of the road to examine this one with interest. In her own mind she had imagined a huddle of small, rough huts, but this extensive place did not come into that category.

At a glance it appeared to be a two-storeyed home with a long line of veranda-fronted doors attached to it. Later she was to learn that each of those doors opened into a self-contained motel unit, and that the ground floor of the house was occupied by Beryl Gibson and her husband Roy who were managing the lodge.

The upper floor was an apartment lived in by Grant Armitage and his small daughter, Jodie. 'Grant owns the place,' Beryl had said. 'He has a law practice in Taupo while we run this place for him and keep an eye on young Jodie. They have dinner with us each evening and that's when we discuss the affairs of the fishing lodge.'

Was there a Mrs Armitage? Donna wondered. Beryl had made no mention of her.

She drove on until she reached the driveway which curved away from the road, then skirted the width of the buildings before turning back to the road. A door marked

'Office' caught her eye, and, leaving the car, she went in and pressed an electric bell. Moments later Beryl came out to greet her.

Beryl was roundly built and in her mid-fifties. Her fair hair was carefully groomed and her blue eyes twinkled with pleasure as they rested upon Donna. 'I'm glad you found your way here,' she smiled. 'Drive your car round to the back of the lodge. Put it in the wide garage near the trees and then come in through the back door. I'll be in the kitchen. There's a tourist coach due and I must attend to the scones. Some of them stop here for a cup of tea.'

Donna obeyed, following the tarmac strip to the back of the building, where an extensive gravelled yard provided parking for cars and boat trailers. It was bordered by maple trees that made a spectacular show of brilliant autumn colours, while nearer the house there were gardens ablaze with dahlias, zinnias, salvia bonfire and giant orange and yellow marigolds. In a grove of trees she caught sight of a stainless steel bench and trough which, she guessed, must be a place for cleaning fish, but there would be plenty of time to examine these things later.

The sound of voices led her towards the large and well equipped kitchen where Beryl was being assisted by an attractive Maori girl whom Donna judged to be about nineteen years of age. Beryl introduced them. 'This is Kiri—Donna. Kiri's my "right-hand man." I couldn't do without her.'

Kiri's skin was the colour of coffee with a good dash of cream, and her large brown eyes glowed with interest at they rested upon Donna. She smiled shyly at Beryl's praise, then began lifting cups from the dishwasher. 'You don't take any notice of her,' she commented. 'It's just that she's got kind words for everyone.'

'Not quite everyone,' Beryl retorted grimly. 'Some of those men who leave their rooms in a pigsty of spilled beer, dirty wet towels on the floor, sodden fishy newspapers on the beds, get a real tongue-bashing from me.'

Kiri laughed. 'Only trouble is, it's beneath your breath and they don't hear a word of it.'

'The day will come when someone gets a real earful,' Beryl threatened as she took a pack of scones from the deep freeze. It was opened at the sink bench where each one was dunked swiftly under running water before being placed on two oven trays.

Donna echoed her surprise. 'Well—I've never seen that done before now.'

Kiri said, 'A short time in the warm oven brings them back to new.'

'These are my emergency scones,' Beryl explained to Donna. 'Normally I like to serve them freshly baked, but today I've been thrown out of gear by young Jodie.'

'Oh?' Donna's delicately arched brows rose a fraction.

'Didn't I tell you Grant has a daughter? She turned six last month. Quite a handful at times.'

'Yes—you mentioned her.'

'She's been a real little cross-patch all day.' Beryl said.

'It really started yesterday,' Kiri reminded her.

'That's right,' Beryl agreed. 'When she got off the school bus yesterday afternoon she began whining and grizzling and complaining of a sore head. Can you imagine a six year old with a headache? I tried to put her to bed, but would she go? Not likely. She declared her head ached because the school bus had been rattling so loudly.'

Kiri gave a short laugh. 'Her father got her to bed right smartly,' she reminded Beryl. 'When he came home he had her between the sheets in a flash. He stands no nonsense from her. Sometimes I think he's too tough on her. After all, she's only a little girl.' The soft Maori voice was full of sympathy.

'I wouldn't advise letting him hear you say so,' Beryl advised.

Donna hesitated for a moment before asking, 'Hasn't the child got a mother?'

Beryl sniffed. 'There was a time when she had a mother—but she up and left. We don't risk our jobs by even the mere mention of her name, so please don't start asking question about *her*.'

'I see. It sounds bad.'

'It was bad, and if you don't mind I'd prefer to change the subject. Now, let me see how those scones are doing——'

At that moment the back door opened to admit a grey-haired man of about sixty. He was short and sturdily built, the lines on his face indicating exposure to sun and wind.

Beryl made the introduction. 'This is my husband, Roy Gibson—and this is Donna Dalrymple.'

Roy ran appreciative grey eyes over Donna's slim form. He grinned cheerfully as he said, 'Beryl told me you were coming. Aren't you forty-second cousins—or something?'

Donna's smile lit her face. 'Probably—or something. Apart from Dad's cousin in Auckland, Beryl's the only relative I've ever found. I haven't worked out exactly how we're connected.'

'You'll be staying with us for a while?' Roy queried. 'What are your plans?'

'I'm really on annual leave,' Donna explained. 'It's now over a year since I came up from Dunedin, and so far I've seen very little of the North Island. I thought I'd drive from Auckland to Wanganui, and then over to New Plymouth.'

'How long do you have?'

'Three weeks, but by taking my holiday now I'm able to add a few extra days for the Easter break.'

'That'll give you time to see something of the country,' Roy agreed, 'and surely it'll give you time to spend a few days with us.'

'It's very kind of you,' Donna said gratefully. 'I'd love to stay for a few days—that's if you're sure Mr Armitage won't mind.'

'Grant? Of course he won't mind.' Beryl exclaimed. 'Roy and I can have guests staying with us any time we wish. We have our own spare room.' She removed the scones from the oven, then broke them open to cool before each one was buttered.

'I wish I could do something to help,' Donna offered as she watched Kiri put dabs of whipped cream on to jam-covered pikelets.

'Everything is under control,' Kiri assured her cheerfully. 'The sandwiches are already made and at the counter in the next room.'

'How's the young one?' Roy asked. 'Is she still complaining about a headache?'

Beryl frowned. 'I haven't heard about it this afternoon but her eyes are watering and she seems to have a very snuffly nose.'

'Do you think she's caught a dose of 'flu from somewhere?' he enquired anxiously.

'It's possible. I told Grant she should be kept in bed. She'll stay there for *him*, but not for *me*, you understand. So he gave her the order and that's where she is—upstairs in bed.'

'*I am not*,' declared a husky voice from behind them.

They turned to regard the pyjama-clad figure of the little girl who stood in the doorway. She had large hazel eyes, short carroty hair and a flushed face which indicated she was not at all well.

'Go back to bed at once,' Beryl ordered sternly.

The child ignored her and crossed the room to stand before Donna. 'Who are you?' she demanded, staring upward.

'I'm Donna. Are you Jodie?'

Jodie nodded and Donna was assailed by the uncanny feeling that she was looking at herself when about that age. There was the same carroty hair she'd hated so much—and the freckles that had dotted her own nose and cheeks, and suddenly her heart went out to the child.

'Shouldn't you be in bed?' she asked quietly.

'I've finished all my orange drink. I want more,' Jodie mumbled in a hoarse voice, then became shaken by a spasm of hard, dry coughing that sounded like a deep bark.

'That's a nasty cough,' Donna said as she placed a hand on the pink forehead. 'It's possible you're running a temperature.' She turned to Beryl. 'Have you a thermometer?'

Beryl shook her head. 'No—I'm afraid the last time it was used it dropped in the basin.'

Jodie coughed again. Her eyes watered and she rubbed a sleeve across her nose. 'I'm thirsty—I want a drink——'

Kiri sent a smile towards Donna. 'You offered to help, so see if you can get her back into bed. We've had trouble keeping her there. You'll find a jug of orange drink in the fridge upstairs.'

At that moment a sound from outside caught their ears. It brought an exclamation from Beryl. 'There's the coach—it *would* come right now. Is that urn boiling, Roy?'

'Don't worry about Jodie, I'll take care of her,' Donna promised.

'Bless you.' Beryl sighed with relief as she followed Kiri and Roy into the next room.

Donna had already glanced through the door to where there were tables, chairs and a glass cabinet for holding food. There was equipment for serving tea and coffee, and, as she now had a quick glimpse of Beryl becoming busy, she felt a rising surge of indignation against Grant Armitage.

Who did he think he was? OK, so he was the boss, but it was too much to expect Beryl to run his motels, serve teas to passing tourists and at the same time attend to his child. It would be interesting to see if he came home at a respectable hour to take at least some responsibility of Jodie—or did he spend time socialising with his cronies in Taupo?

And the child's mother was not to be mentioned. That was pretty rich, Donna decided. What sort of a life had he dished out to her? *Why* had she up and left him, as Beryl had put it? The answers to these questions would be most interesting, Donna thought as she followed Jodie upstairs.

But her thoughts were running away with her and she pulled them together with a jerk. There are two sides to every question, she reminded herself in an effort to be fair, yet despite this fact she found she was beginning to thoroughly dislike Grant Armitage before she had even set eyes on him. And she also knew she was being a fool to wonder about him at all.

Nevertheless she found herself interested in the way the upper floor of the obviously old house and been converted into his living quarters. Apart from the kitchen and bathroom, and the laundry area where fishing gear was also kept, the entire floor was covered by a carpet of deep cream natural sheepskin which gave an immediate feeling of luxury.

In the spacious living-room the contrasting dark red settee and easy chairs offered comfort. A round pedestal dining-table, its chairs tucked neatly beneath it, stood in the centre of the room, while a television set, sideboard and cocktail cabinet were in convenient places against the walls. At one end, the room extended into an alcove to contain a large desk and the telephone, but it was the lack of flowers and the type of books on the shelves that made Donna decide it was essentially a man's room.

At the far end of the room were wide sliding glass doors which opened on to a balcony, and, passing through them, she stood to gaze at the extensive views towards the three mountains and across the lake towards the distant lines of hills. Then, below her to the right, she found she could look down on the row of motels that comprised Aubrey's Place.

She left the balcony and crossed the living-room to the passageway which gave access to the other rooms. In the largest, which also looked out on the lake, she caught a glimpse of a dull gold bedspread and matching curtains, while the second room featured curtains and bedcover in a deep turquoise shade.

Jodie pulled at her sleeve. 'I sleep in here,' she informed Donna as she led her into the smallest room where the bedspread and curtains were blue, and where the bed presented a tumbled mass of disarranged blankets, sheets, colouring books, spilled crayons and several dolls in various stages of dress and undress.

Donna removed the dolls and books, shook the blankets free of crayons and remade the bed.

Jodie watched her for a moment, then picked up the largest doll. 'This is Lulu. She's the boss because she tells the others what to do.'

Donna turned back the sheet then looked at Lulu's round, blue eyes in her beautiful face. 'She's very pretty. Can you hear what she's saying right now?'

Jodie's eyes widened as she said uncertainly. 'No, what is she saying?'

'She's telling *you* what to do. She's saying *you* must get into bed and stay there—but first your face and hands will be washed.'

*'She is not saying that!'* Jodie protested rebelliously.

'Yes, she is—it's coming through loud and clear,' Donna asserted. She then shepherded the child to the bathroom, which was modern with its tiles, shower cubicle, bath and mirrors.

A short time later Jodie was tucked into bed and, as she looked up at Donna, she pleaded in a pathetic voice, 'Will you stay with me? I'm—I'm so lonely all by myself—and I'm still very thirsty.'

'Of course—I'll find you a drink.' She went into the kitchen where she was faced by white cupboards, a stainless steel bench and sink, a combination fridge and deep freeze and a dishwasher. It was a kitchen to satisfy most wives, so why wasn't there one here?

As Kiri had said there was a jug of orange drink in the fridge, and she carried it back to the bedroom to be met by more pleading.

'Please, promise to stay with me——' The lower lip quivered.

'I'll stay for a while,' Donna promised, then, looking at the floor she added, 'I'd better pick up these crayons before they become trodden into the carpet.'

She went down on her hands and knees to find small broken pieces that had rolled beneath the bed, some of them being so far under she had to lie on her stomach to reach them, and she was in this recumbent position when a deep voice spoke from the doorway.

It echoed surprise as it demanded, 'Who on earth are you?'

'She's Donna,' Jodie explained.

Donna pulled her head from beneath the bed, then scrambled to her feet to face the tall man who had entered the room. She noticed that she came no higher than his shoulder, and she was immediately conscious that here was a handsome man of athletic build. For a moment she was lost for words, then, in an attempt to regain her dignity she tried to explain, 'There are crayons under the bed. Unless they're found they'll disappear into the vacuum cleaner.'

She then became aware that he was staring at her with varying expressions that changed from amazement to distrust, and that there was suspicion lurking in the dark grey eyes that had narrowed as they swept over her, taking in every detail of her appearance. The colour of her auburn hair came in for special attention, and from

beneath his dark brows his eyes had almost turned to slits
as they rested upon her slightly retroussée nose and
generous mouth.

'She's Donna,' Jodie said again.

'OK, so you're Donna,' he gritted as though having
taken a sudden dislike to her. 'Donna who—may I ask?'

His entire attitude niggled at her, getting beneath her
skin and filling her with the desire to attack. Her chin
rose slightly as she snapped back at him, 'Do you always
demand identification in such a rude and arrogant
manner, Mr Armitage? I presume you *are* Mr
Armitage?'

'Of course I'm Armitage——'

She cut in. 'Does it not occur to you that someone who
has been attending to your daughter deserves a little
more courtesy than you appear to be capable of
showing?'

Jodie chimed in, 'She washed my face and hands,
Daddy.'

He ignored both Donna's accusation and the child's
information as he frowned and rasped. 'You still haven't
told me who you are.'

Perversity kept her silent on that point. 'It can't
possibly interest you. However what *should* be of concern
to you at the moment is the state of your daughter's
health.'

He sent a brief glance towards Jodie. 'Obviously she's
suffering from a bout of 'flu. She'll be better tomorrow, or
the next day.'

'You're sure about that?'

'Of course. Children go up and down like bouncing
balls.'

'An authority, are you, Mr Armitage?'

He frowned. 'She doesn't look too bad to me.'

'I don't want to worry you, Mr Armitage—but I fear it
could be a little more serious than a mere bout of 'flu.'

'You don't worry me at all, Miss Whoever-you-are.

She'll be back at school tomorrow or the day after.'

Donna was irritated by his complacency and her voice became cold as she said, 'Mr Armitage, are you being deliberately obtuse, or is it that you're too busy to observe the situation?'

A pathetic voice came from the bed. 'Beryl says my daddy just lives at the office.'

He smiled at the child. 'But I come home to you every evening, don't I? And aren't I with you at weekends? You know I love you.'

Jodie noded. 'Sometimes you bring me a present.' She looked at him hopefully. 'You gotta pressy for me this time?'

He shook his head. 'You'll have to wait till Thursday and then we'll see about an Easter egg.'

Donna sent him a cool stare. 'She may not be feeling like chocolate eggs later this week, Mr Armitage.'

He gave a snort of amusement. 'That'll be the day——'

'Perhaps we should discuss it in the next room.' She swept past him, and as she did so she became acutely conscious that here was a man with something vital about him. However, the thought was brushed from her mind as he came to stand beside her at the glass doors.

'Well, what more have you to say, Miss Whoever?'

Her eyes were thoughtful as they stared at the waters breaking along the narrow shore. 'Very little—apart from suggesting you call a doctor for Jodie.'

His voice became scathing. 'Obviously, you have no idea how difficult it is to get doctors to make house calls—and as for dragging one half-way down the lakeside to visit a child with a mere cold—well, you'd have to be joking.'

She became impatient. 'I've told you it could be more than a mere cold.'

'Your diagnosis being—what?' His tone dripped sarcasm.

'Measles.'

'*Measles*?' He was startled enough to echo the word. 'What makes you think so?'

'The symptoms, of course. That particular hard dry cough, for one thing. It's enough to make me very suspicious.'

'Are you a nurse that you're so knowledgeable?'

'No, but working in a doctor's surgery keeps me from being completely ignorant about such matters.' She fell silent, annoyed with herself for having imparted that piece of information.

'For whom do you work?' he asked casually.

She smiled sweetly. 'Does it matter?'

'Not the slightest iota,' he snapped, his mouth becoming a thin line as his jaw hardened.

The signs of his barely concealed irritation were not lost on her, and suddenly it seemed as if the very sight of her was making him more bad-tempered every moment. In short, she was someone he'd rather not look at. And this, if she intended to stay with Beryl for a few days, could be the cause of discomfort—especially if he and Jodie were in the habit of having their evening meal with Beryl and Roy.

The situation called for a change of attitude between them, and in an effort to clear the atmosphere she forced herself to say amicably, 'There are cars parked outside the back doors of the motels. It's a pity one of them doesn't belong to a doctor.'

Startled, he turned to look at her. 'By Jove—it's not impossible because Beryl said Doc Fraser from Hamilton had booked in. He usually comes late in the afternoon and he's never without his little black bag. I wonder if he's arrived.'

Jodie's voice called from the bedroom. 'Donna— Donna—you promised you'd stay with me——'

Donna went to the child's bedroom door. 'I'm still here, Jodie, but Daddy's home now. You won't need me while he's here.'

'I do—I do—I want you to stay——' It was a wail that ended in tears, accompanied by a bout of coughing.

Donna turned to Grant. 'Have you any tissues? She really needs them for her eyes and nose.'

'I'll see if Beryl can find a box—and if there's any sign of Doc Fraser.' He strode towards a door at the end of the passage.

Following to see where it led, Donna learnt it was the apartment's back entrance where a flight of steps left a landing and went down to the parking area at the back of the building.

She then shepherded Jodie to the toilet, gave her another drink and completed her former tidying of the room. She was again on the floor searching for crayons when she heard voices in the living-room, and she sprang to her feet as Grant ushered an elderly man into the bedroom.

Grant's introduction was brief. 'This is Doctor Fraser—Donna.'

Doc Fraser was a cheerful man who appeared to be edging towards sixty. He acknowledged Donna with a nod, then went to the bedside.

'Well, now—what have we here?' he asked Jodie in a soft voice that retained the remains of a Scottish accent. 'Are you the sick bairn—or is it this dolly?'

'This is Lulu, but she's quite well,' Jodie informed him as she became shaken by a spasm of coughing which was followed by a sneeze.

The box of tissues in Grant's hand caught Donna's eye. She took it from him and extracted several to wipe Jodie's eyes and nose.

Doc Fraser took a thermometer from his bag. 'Are you old enough to hold this under your tongue without biting it?' he asked Jodie.

'Course I am—I'm six now,' she mumbled indignantly.

Half a minute later he looked at it and frowned.

Grant, leaning his long length against the doorway

said lazily, 'Am I right, Doc? It's nothing more than a dose of 'flu? Donna imagines it could be measles,' he added with an amused laugh.

'I'm afraid she might be correct.' The doctor's sharp blue eyes stared intently at Donna. 'What made you pick on measles?'

She smiled. 'I've heard that dry bark of a cough before today.'

'Donna's working in a doctor's surgery,' Grant put in slyly.

Doc Fraser was interested. 'You're working here in Taupo?'

'No, I'm in Auckland,' was all she said.

'Really? who are you with up there, may I ask?'

'Doctor Frank Dalrymple,' she felt compelled to admit.

'Ah—I know him. And I also know the other Dalrymple, his cousin in Dunedin. We went through medical school together.'

'You know my father?' Her eyes shone as the words slipped out before she could stop them.

'If your father is Alexander Dalrymple—then yes, I know him. He's one of Dunedin's finest surgeons.'

Pride caused her to take a deep breath. Fancy Father's reputation being known so far away in the North Island! She glanced at Grant Armitage and was shocked to see the expression on his face. What was it? Sneering contempt—or something worse, like utter hatred? Ignoring it, she turned to Doc Fraser. 'So, how do we cope with measles?'

He sighed. 'I'm afraid that isolation is the name of the game. She must be kept in bed, with somebody around to see that she does just that. Some children are difficult to keep in bed.'

'She'll do as she's told,' Grant said gruffly.

Doc Fraser went on, 'And she must be given a nourishing diet of soups and milk puddings. Glucose is always a help. When did she begin to cough?'

'This morning,' Grant told him gloomily. 'There was also a great deal of sneezing.'

'Then you can expect the red spots to come out in about four days. You'll find them popping up on her brow to begin with, and then on her cheeks and chin. Nice little groups of them——'

'This isolation business—how long does it last?' Grant had begun to look thoroughly worried.

'It can end ten days after the rash has appeared, so long as all fever, catarrh and mucous discharges have disappeared.'

'But—that'll be a fortnight!' Grant Armitage's voice echoed his dismay.

'Aye, laddie, it will.' The doctor looked at him with a stern glint in his eyes. 'You understand that the child will need constant attention, I presume?'

'I'm not so dumb that I'm unable to see that,' Grant retorted in rumbling tones that betrayed his irritation.

Doc Fraser frowned. 'How shall you manage? I've been coming to this place long enough to know that Beryl has her hands full—and I doubt that she can spare Kiri.'

Grant's lips became compressed. 'We'll manage somehow,' he declared stubbornly. 'I'll hire a nurse.'

Doc Fraser gave a short laugh. 'You'll find a nurse at the drop of a hat in a place like Taupo? I've heard of other people trying to do that and they've had no luck at all. Taupo is a holiday resort. People come to enjoy themselves rather than to become cooped up with measles.' His piercing blue eyes turned upon Donna. 'What are you doing here? On holiday, are you?'

She nodded. 'Yes. I've just begun my annual leave by having a few days with Beryl. She's a distant relative.'

'Perhaps Grant can persaude you to stay longer.'

'I'd—I'd have to think about it,' she said evasively, darting a quick glance at the tall, dark man who looked anything but pleased by the suggestion. 'In any case, Mr

Armitage is sure to know of some person who would come and stay with Jodie.'

'Do you, Grant?' The doctor shot the question at him.

He shook his head, then ran fingers through his hair. 'No not a confounded soul——'

Jodie began to cry. 'You—you promised to stay with me,' she sobbed pathetically to Donna. 'I—I don't want anyone else——' The words ended in a hoarse croak.

Donna tried to comfort the child. 'I'm sure your father can find somebody to stay with you.'

'No—no—*I want you*——' she wailed, then began to cough.

'She'll stay with you,' Doc Fraser assured the child with confidence as he grinned at Donna.

'What makes you so sure about that?' Grant drawled. 'I don't know this young woman. Until you dragged the information out of her I didn't even know her surname, so why the devil should she ruin her vacation by staying here?'

The doctor smiled. 'At a guess, I'd say she'll stay because she's Alexander Dalrymple's daughter.'

'What's he got to do with the situation?' Grant snapped.

'It's all a matter of character, laddie. She'll stay because she can see the child needs her help and because she knows it's the right thing to do. You see, I know her parents, and I believe that this type of character will have been born and bred in her.'

Donna laughed. 'You're being very cunning, Doctor Fraser,' she accused. 'You're not telling these things to Mr Armitage, you're pointing them out to *me* so that I'll feel obliged to stay, otherwise my parents will be disappointed in me. I'd be letting them down.'

Doc Fraser grinned. 'I can see you're no fool, lassie. Your mother was always quick on the uptake, too. I recall it didn't take her long to recognise a good man when she met your father——'

'These reminiscences are most touching,' Grant interrupted with a touch of sarcasm. 'However, you appear to be forgetting the compromising situation it would put her in. It means she'll have to stay in this apartment—alone—with me.'

'Rubbish. It's no more compromising than if she'd been a fully trained nurse.' He turned to Donna. 'Have you had nursing experience, my dear?'

'Only a little. First aid, and so forth. My father insisted upon it. He was rather keen for me to take up nursing.'

The doctor's eyes turned towards Grant. 'Well, there you are. What more can you wish for?'

Grant Armitage glared at Donna in cold silence, his suppressed anger being mute evidence of his quandary.

His ungracious manner incensed Donna to the extent of making her say, 'I can tell you what more he could wish for, Doctor Fraser. He'd prefer to see somebody else—no matter who—in my place. It's true that we've only just met, but for some unknown reason he's taken a dislike to me on sight.'

The doctor was shocked. 'Surely you're exaggerating.'

'No, I am not,' she vowed. 'Ask him about it yourself, and see if you can find out why my appearance offends him.'

Doc Fraser sent questioning eyes towards Grant. 'I can hardly believe *that*. Is it true, laddie?'

There was no reply.

# CHAPTER TWO

DONNA sent a triumphant look towards Doc Fraser. 'There now, doesn't his attitude speak for itself? Not that I *care*, of course. He means nothing to me—absolutely *nothing*,' she added vehemently.

At the same time she realised that while her own appearance obviously offended him, *his* appearance did nothing to offend her. He was a handsome man, she admitted to herself. There *could* be laughter crinkles about his eyes, and there *could* be lines of humour about his mouth, but at the moment they had been eradicated by his inner frustration and undisguised anger at the thought of being lumbered with herself. And then her eyes widened as she listened to the man's next words.

'You should be able to see for yourself,' he snapped at Doc Fraser who was still waiting for an explanation.

The blue eyes sent him a penetrating stare. *'See?* I see the daughter of my old friends Alex and Marie—and that's all.'

'I can see more than that,' Grant retorted enigmatically. 'And so can you, if only you'd admit it.'

The exchange bewildered Donna. She had already grasped that it was her appearance that had raised Grant Armitage's antagonism, but what more could there be? Her clothes, perhaps? Was her green jersey stretched too tightly across her breasts, accentuating them more clearly than necessary? Was he a man who objected to trews on a woman? There was nothing loud about the blue and green MacKay tartan—so what was bugging him?

She flicked a glance at his own clothes, noticing that they were formal and eminently suitable for interviewing clients in his law office. His collar and tie remained unloosened while the jacket of his well cut, dark-grey suit did nothing to disguise the broadness of his shoulders.

Doc Fraser sighed then shook his head lugubriously. 'I can diagnose the child, but the father's state evades me. Would you lie down on your back and open your mouth wide, laddie? I'll try to take a wee peep at your brains—if they're there.'

Grant snorted. 'You're allowed to have your little joke, Doc—and I'm mighty grateful you were here to look at Jodie.'

'That's all right.' The older man left the bedside abruptly, then paused as a thought struck him. 'By the way, have either of you had measles?'

'Yes, years ago when I was a child,' Donna said. 'I doubt that I'll get them again.'

'Ditto,' Grant said crisply.

'Good.' He glanced from one to the other. 'You won't forget what I said about isolation and the fact that the child will need to have somebody with her?'

The remark caused Grant to frown at the carpet, while Donna left the bedroom to stare unseeingly through the living-room window set on the north wall beside the sliding doors. Could she bear to spend the isolation period with this man? She doubted it. She knew that Grant Armitage had accompanied Doc Fraser down the stairs, and, while the main purpose of the doctor's visit had been Jodie, she guessed that she herself was now the subject of their discussion. The mumble of their voices could be heard momentarily, and although she longed to know what was being said about her, not one word of it reached her ears.

The sound of weeping took her back to the bedroom and, as she looked at the small flushed face, she was overcome by sympathy. Then, as she used tissues on the watering eyes and nose, she knew she was trapped by her own pity. She knew that even if the father hated her, for some unfathomable reason she'd stay for Jodie's sake.

After all, what did *he* matter? It was the child who mattered. She couldn't care less about *him*. In fact, it might be fun to stay just—just to annoy him. How *dared* he treat her as though she was something not to be touched for fear of contamination?

A short time later Donna leaned over the railing of the inside stairway while Beryl stood in the hall below. 'What's the story?' the latter asked, her round face showing concern.

Donna was surprised. 'Didn't Mr Armitage tell you?'

Beryl shook her head. 'No. He strode past without speaking to me. I wondered if I'd offended him in some way.'

'It's natural for him to be upset. Jodie has measles.'

Beryl was aghast. '*Measles*—and the place booked out for Easter. What on earth shall we do?'

'Doctor Fraser says she must be kept isolated, especially at this particular period before the spots come out.'

'It looks as if I'll be well and truly on the run,' Beryl exclaimed. 'I'll be running up and down stairs and running the place as well.'

'Have you had measles?' Donna asked.

Beryl shook her head. 'I don't think so. I can't remember that I ever had them as a child.'

'Then you'd be wise to stay downstairs. Mr Armitage won't be amused if you catch them. What about Kiri?'

'I think she's had measles. She seemed to recognise all that snuffling and sneezing as something she herself had experienced.' Distress echoed from Beryl's voice as she wailed, '*What are we going to do?*'

'Don't worry, you've got me. I'll stay until the worst is over.'

'Oh, my dear, I'm so sorry. This will completely ruin your holiday—the first you've had in the North Island.'

Donna smiled down at her. 'I've a strong suspicion I'll

be replaced before very long. Mr Armitage appears to have taken a dislike to me.'

Beryl's jaw sagged slightly. '*Dislike*? What are you talking about? Surely it's something you're imagining.'

'I am not. You've heard of love at first sight—well, meet a victim of *hate* at first sight.'

Beryl was shocked. 'That's ridiculous. Why should he hate you?'

Donna shrugged. 'Your guess is as good as mine.'

An expression that was almost one of enlightenment hovered across Beryl's face. 'Surely he wouldn't——' she began, then fell silent.

'Surely he wouldn't what?' Donna urged.

But Beryl shook her head. 'No, it's just my silly imagination. He couldn't possibly——'

'Please tell me, Beryl,' Donna pleaded. 'It might not be your imagination, and if I'm to stay up here I'd like to know what he has against me—especially as he's never set eyes on me before.'

'Hasn't he? He might be looking upon you as a ghost from the past——' Beryl stopped as though fearing she'd said too much.

'What are you talking about?'

But Beryl only laughed, although to Donna's ears it sounded somewhat forced. 'Forget it, my dear,' she advised. 'I doubt that his bad mood had anything to do with you. Things might have gone wrong with one of his law cases. Perhaps a client didn't tell him all that should have been told. It does happen, you know.'

But Donna wasn't convinced. No matter how awry a case had gone it would not have turned his grey eyes so cold and hard when they had rested upon her. However, before she could put this thought into words a plaintive voice floated from the bedroom.

'Donna—Donna—I'm thirsty——'

A short time after she had attended to the child, Roy carried her suitcase upstairs. 'We didn't expect to land you slap-bang into this kind of mess,' he said apologetically, 'but I can tell you we're mightly grateful you're here, and even more thankful to know you'll stay and help us out.'

Donna smiled and said nothing, her thoughts going to Grant Armitage whose gratitude appeared to be non-existent.

'Beryl says you'll find towels and linen for the guest room in the hall cupboard,' Roy informed her. 'And there are changes of sheets if the young one needs them. And she says there are prepared pies and dinners in the deep freeze. All you have to do is heat them in the oven. Do you think you can manage?'

'Of course. Tell her I'll find everything.'

'And she sent this small piece of fresh fish to be steamed for Jodie—if she'll eat it.'

'I'll try and get it into her. Tell Beryl not to worry about a single thing.'

'I'll do that, but naturally she's in a state about it all.'

'Poor Beryl, she has so much to do——'

'When we're really busy Kiri's mother comes in to give a hand, and when that happens I'm not sure who's boss in the kitchen. But at the moment you're the biggest godsend I've seen for a long time.'

When Roy went downstairs Donna examined the contents of the deep freeze. She decided to use a pack marked 'beef casserole with vegetables', a flat, oblong pack labelled 'apple strudel' and a carton of ice cream. Jodie, she felt sure, would manage a little ice cream, and if Mr Armitage deigned to join her for a meal he would not go hungry.

She then found sheets and made up the bed in the spare room. Her clothes were hung in the wardrobe, and she was in the midst of arranging her make-up on the dressing-table when she happened to look up and see his face reflected in the mirror. She paused, staring at him transfixed.

His voice held irony. 'You're settling in, I see.'

'You'd rather I didn't do so?' she asked without turning round. 'I can easily remove myself if you've found someone to take care of Jodie. Just say the word and I'll be gone in a flash.'

He stared at her without speaking, and in the mirror she watched his eyes travel over her figure as though examining her shoulders, her tartan-covered buttocks and legs.

'Well, have you found someone?' she asked, turning round to face him.

'No, actually I haven't—although I'll admit I rushed to Taupo to see if any of my friends knew of someone who could come here.'

'Couldn't you have phoned them?'

'And let you hear me being turned down flat? That would have given you a good laugh.'

'So you drew a blank?' she asked, showing a polite but exaggerated interest.

'Most of them thought it hilarious that I imagined anyone with an Easter break would toss it to the winds.'

'Really? And you found that surprising, Mr Armitage?'

He sent her a hard and penetrating stare. 'It makes me wonder why you should be so anxious to toss your own holiday to the winds.'

'You've got it wrong, Mr Armitage. I'm not at all anxious, as you suggest. It's just that I've found myself in a position where a child and a relative need my assistance.'

'You're looking upon Jodie as a relative?'

'Of course not. I mean Beryl.'

He regarded her in silence for several moments, then asked, 'What relation is Beryl to you?'

'She's a sort of cousin. I haven't had time to work it out because I've met her only once before today.'

'And Carmen—what relation is *she* to you?' The

question was shot at her in a harsh voice.

She stared at him blankly. *'Carmen?* Who is Carmen?'

He uttered a mirthless laugh. 'Huh! As though you don't know!'

She shook her head in bewildered silence.

'So that's it, is it? You intend to play dumb about Carmen.'

She lost patience. 'You're out of your mind, Mr Armitage.'

His eyes narrowed as they surveyed her features. 'Are you a cousin or a sister I haven't heard about?'

She felt he was dissecting her face piece by piece. 'You're raving,' she retorted angrily. 'I haven't got a sister, or a brother. If you doubt me it should be easy enough to check.'

The close scrutiny of her face had embarrassed her, especially as she watched his eyes linger upon her lips. She felt a flush creeping into her cheeks and, before it could cover her face in a vivid crimson, she brushed past him and went to the kitchen where she peeped into the oven.

He followed her. 'That smells good,' he remarked, watching her from the doorway.

'Beryl said to help myself from the deep freeze. The oven's on a fairly low heat so you can have a meal when it suits you—unless you'd prefer to eat downstairs,' she added casually.

He made no reply while seeming to continue his scrutiny of her face, her hair and her figure.

Ignoring it she said, 'Incidentally, I don't think Beryl has had measles. I know it's a childhood complaint, but adults can catch it. Nor do I know if you could pass on the infection, but it would be a pity to hand it to her on a plate.'

The grin on his face changed his entire expression. 'You're saying you'd like me to eat with you?'

She bristled. 'Your ego does you credit. I'm merely

pointing out that if Beryl catches measles it will be most awkward for the fishing lodge. Aubrey's Place will suffer.'

He became serious. 'You're right. Perhaps I could sprinkle a few germs about the table. I'll eat up here until the worst is over.'

'What about carrying infection to the office?' she asked thoughtfully.

'Oh, there's no worry on that score. The law offices have a good break at Easter; at least ten days if you count the Easter period.'

'*Ten days*——' she echoed is dismay.

He frowned at her. 'The idea of being cooped up with me for ten days appears to horrify you.'

'It certainly does, Mr Armitage,' she snapped vehemently.

'That's strange. I was under the impression you'd come here to observe—yet when presented with this golden opportunity——'

She was nonplussed, her hazel eyes widening slightly as they searched his face for an answer. 'Observe what, for Pete's sake?'

'The general situation, of course. Naturally—on Carmen's behalf. No doubt she sent you.'

'You're raving again, Mr Armitage.' She turned away from him and began to prepare a small amount of fish for Jodie. Fortunately the task needed little concentration because her mind was filled with one single question. *Who was Carmen?*

She was unable to recall anyone of that name, and further—why should there be any connection between this person and herself? But suddenly she became impatient with her own nagging thoughts, and, brushing the question aside, she went to attend to the child. Here she found that persuasion was needed before Jodie would eat the fish, but to her relief it eventually disappeared.

When she returned to the living-room she found he

had poured her a sherry. 'Thank you,' she murmured, surprised by this unexpected affability.

'It might help to thaw that ball of ice you've got tucked inside,' he remarked sardonically.

She regarded him steadily. 'You're suggesting I'm a cold type of person? Coming from you, that's mighty rich,' she retorted as she carried the sherry to the window where she stood gazing out into the semi-darkness. On the highway, passing cars followed the bright beams of their headlights, while out on the lake flashes of red and green port and starboard lights indicated the return of launches manned by fishermen who had waited to catch the evening rise.

He said, 'Would you be good enough to sit down and tell me about yourself? We might as well get things straight.'

His tone held a command that caused her to bristle, therefore she kept her back to him. 'What is there to get straight? There's nothing about me that can possible interest you, therefore why should I tell you anything?'

'That's where you're wrong.' His tone was clipped.

She swung round to face him. 'Mr Armitage, you've made no secret of disliking me from—from the first moment of clapping eyes on me. OK—you're at liberty to do so, but please don't expect me to—to bubble over with friendship and to become confidential with a man who regards me as—as something he's dragged up from the bottom of the lake.'

Anger forced her to gulp her sherry. To have a man look upon her with suspicion and contempt was a new experience, and the knowledge that this was now the case filled her with frustration. *Drat* him, why should she care what he thought? Her hand holding the empty glass shook slightly.

She also knew he was standing behind her, watching her intently, because she could see his reflection in the plate glass of the side window. And then she saw him return to the cocktail cabinet, pick up the decanter and refill her glass.

As he did so he gave a sigh that betrayed exasperation. 'I wish you'd sit down and relax. I feel uncomfortable lounging in a chair while a woman stands.'

'Very well.' At least he has a few manners, she thought as she chose the rocking-chair near the sliding doors.

He sat opposite in a high-backed wing chair, watching while she sipped the sherry. 'Feeling better?' he asked after a long pause during which his eyes hardly left her face.

'I suppose so,' she admitted grudgingly. Strangely, the silence between them had become almost companionable. Or was the sherry merely smoothing her ruffled feathers?

He leaned his head against the back of the chair, regarding her from beneath lowered lids. 'So—if you live away down south in Dunedin, what brings you to the North Island and such a distance from home?'

'Relations, mainly. The search for family.' The words were out before she could control them. The sherry was loosening her tongue. Well, what of it? She had nothing to hide.

But apparently he thought otherwise because his eyes held a strange glint as he probed. 'Apart from Beryl, you expected to find another relative round these parts?'

The question had been put to her smoothly, yet she sensed the underlying suspicion. Did he imagine she was searching for Carmen—whoever she was? Perhaps it would clear the air between them if she explained her reason for coming north. No doubt it would make her appear immature, but what did that matter? Why should she care what he thought?

Nevertheless she asked casually, 'Do you think it's a weakness to wish to belong to a family?'

He frowned thoughtfully. 'It could show a desire—or perhaps a need—to have people to whom one can cling.'

'Then I suppose I have that need. I've always wanted to belong to a family, but there are only the three of us—Mother, Father and myself.'

'No grandparents? No aunts or uncles?'

'None. And that means no cousins.'

'At least you have your parents.'

She gave a short laugh. 'When I was at home I seldom saw them. Father is an extremely busy man, up to his eyes in surgery. Mother is equally busy, but with bridge, golf and doing what she terms good works on various committees. I've always been very much alone.'

'And very sorry for yourself?' he smiled.

'I wasn't actually *sorry* for myself until I'd been to a school friend's birthday party. She had brothers and sisters, and there were aunts, uncles and cousins who had come to make it a family gathering. Everyone seemed so *happy*, so *glad* to see each other.'

'How old were you at the time?'

'I was twelve, and old enough to recognise the utter loneliness of my own position. That night I told Father I wished we had lots of relations. He laughed and told me to count my blessings, declaring that relatives can be absolute pests.'

Grant stared into his glass. 'He's right. Many people would be better off without some of their relatives.' His tone held a tinge of bitterness.

She sent him a quick glance. 'You have some who annoy you?'

He did not elucidate. Instead he shrugged and said, 'Go on with the story.'

'Well, I pointed out to Father that if anything happened to my parents I wouldn't have a soul who was a relation. I wouldn't have *anyone* I could turn to for comfort. Father laughed. He told me that neither he nor Mother had any intention of shoving off this earth—at least, not for years—and by that time I'd be married with a family of my own.'

He regarded her thoughtfully. 'I suspect you'd like to have a large family.'

'I've been an only child, therefore I don't want to have just *one* child. I'd like to have at least four——' She stopped, appalled to find herself confiding such matters to this man. Her cheeks became hot and when he lifted the decanter from the coffee table between them she placed a hand over the top of her glass. 'No more, thank you. I'm becoming much too talkative.'

'You haven't told me why you came to Auckland.'

'Oh, that was most unexpected. A little over a year ago Father came home and told us that his second cousin, a doctor in Auckland, had registered to attend a medical conference in Dunedin. That evening he phoned and invited him to stay with us. I was amazed because Father had never even mentioned this cousin.'

'This was Frank Dalrymple—the doctor you're working for?'

'Yes. At the time I was working as a receptionist for Father. I attended to his appointments and accounts— the general dogsbody about the place. Father was in the midst of boasting about my capabilities when Frank interrupted him to offer me a job. It happened that his own receptionist was leaving to get married and live in another city. Her position was mine if I wanted it.'

Grant chuckled. 'I'll bet Father was rocked.'

'Rocked? He was floored. At first he was livid, but later he realised it would give me the opportunity to see other parts of New Zealand, especially Auckland. However, that wasn't my real reason for accepting the job.'

'Oh?' There was a sudden watchfulness about him, almost as though he expected her to let something slip.

'He had a family,' she explained simply. 'I wanted to meet them, to get to know them.'

'Ah. You were finding relatives.'

'Family,' she corrected. 'I felt I'd found *family*.'

'And Beryl—where does she come in?'

'I met Beryl when she came in for an injection to help guard against influenza during the winter. Frank introduced her as his cousin, which probably means that her mother was a Dalrymple. She told me about Aubrey's Place, and when she knew I had a vacation due—well, here I am. But that's enough about me, Mr Armitage.'

'Is it necessary for you to keep up this Mr Armitage racket? Can't you call me Grant?'

She sent him a level look, the darkness through the sliding doors throwing shadows into her eyes. 'I doubt it. Your underlying antagonism causes me to think of you only as Mr Armitage. I'd prefer to leave it at that.'

'As you wish—Miss Dalrymple,' he returned stiffly.

She forced herself to smile at him while searching in her mind for a topic of conversation that would lie more in his interest. 'Suppose you tell me about Aubrey's Place,' she suggested. 'Has it always been a fishing lodge?'

'No. This two-storeyed part was once the home of Aubrey Johnson, a retired land developer. Most of his friends were keen fishermen, and many of them formed the habit of dropping in to spend the night at what they called Aubrey's place. In fact, it reached the stage when Aubrey found difficulty in coping with them.'

'He had a wife and children?'

'He had a wife but no children. My father was his closest friend and it was he who suggested building the row of motel units beside the house. In those days they were serviced by Kiri's mother.'

'Then you've been coming here for years?'

'Yes, from the time I was old enough to hold a rod. When Aubrey died my father bought the place from his widow, and I later purchased it from Dad. I wanted to live in it and had no intention of waiting until I'd inherited it.'

'How long have you owned it?' Donna asked casually.

'About seven years.'

'So you wanted to live in it when you married Jodie's mother,' she said with sudden insight.

He stood up abruptly. 'Isn't it time we dragged that food out of the oven?'

'Yes, I'll just have a quick peep at Jodie and then we'll eat.'

She went to the bedroom expecting the little girl to be asleep, but instead of finding closed lids she was greeted by a heavy-eyed stare that came from a face that looked flushed in the dim glow of the bed-side nightlight. And then the question that came hoarsely surprised her.

'Donna, do you know Santa Claus?'

'Well, not personally.'

'I don't mean the ones you see sitting in shops; I mean the *real* Santa with his sleigh and reindeer and—and all the toys in great big bags.'

Donna nodded. 'I know who you mean.'

'How long will it be before he comes again?'

'Oh, a long time. About eight months, because this is only April. But Santa doesn't use his sleigh and reindeer in New Zealand because he comes in the middle of our summer.'

'I suppose he drives a truck,' Jodie said with perception. 'Can he bring *anything* to anyone?'

'Just about anything.' Donna replied warily, wondering where these questions were leading.

Jodie sat up and began to cough. 'I—I want to—to write a letter to him,' she gasped in the midst of the spasm.

Donna applied tissues to the streaming eyes and nose, then poured a drink from the covered jug on the bedside table. 'You can't write a letter tonight. Tomorrow, perhaps——'

'Will you help me—please——?'

'Of course.'

'Do you know how to send it to Santa Claus?'

'I'll have to think about it,' Donna prevaricated. 'Have you something special you want to ask of him?'

Jodie nodded. 'I want him to bring my mother to me. All the girls at school have mothers.'

Donna was at a loss for words. 'You've got Beryl,' she said at last. 'Beryl looks after you like a mother.'

'She's not my mother—and she's bossy. I want my own mother.'

'Well, you've got your father. I'm sure he loves you.'

'He doesn't come home till night time,' Jodie pouted. 'Other fathers are there *all the time*,' she exaggerated.

Grant's voice spoke from behind them, his amused tone softening as he said to Jodie, 'Just you wait till Easter. You'll see me around for days and days——'

Donna smiled at Jodie. 'Now you *really* have something to look forward to.' At the same time she wondered how much the child would see of him. Would he actually sacrifice his fishing? No doubt he'd been looking forward to going out on the lake.

Jodie looked up at him. 'Donna's going to help me write a letter to Santa Claus. It's about my mother——'

His tone became abrupt. 'So I heard. However, I'm afraid you'll have to learn that Santa can't bring all the things we ask for. Now then, be a good girl and go to sleep at once.'

Later, as they sat at the round dining-table he said, 'Don't let the thought of the letter worry you. She'll have forgotten about it by tomorrow morning.'

'And if she hasn't?'

'Then help her write it. The idea will have vanished from her mind by Christmas time.'

'And if it hasn't?' Donna pursued, eyeing him steadily.

'She'll be in for a mighty big disappointment,' he retorted.

'Poor little girl,' Donna sighed. She felt overwhelmed by sympathy for the child.

'It'll be lesson number one in the fact that disappointments are part of this life, Miss Dalrymple. We have to learn to cope with them. Surely you can understand that?'

'I suppose so.' She glanced at him quickly. 'Are you saying you've had more than your share?'

'I've had plenty.' His mouth snapped shut.

'They appear to have made you bitter—and suspicious, I may add. Your attitude towards me is proof enough of *that* particular fact.'

'Perhaps I should explain that your appearance upset me.'

'*Charming*! Gallant as well, I see.'

'You don't understand,' he said ruefully. 'For a moment I thought you were Carmen. You're so very like her.'

'Well, I'm not,' she snapped. 'I'm Donna. Got it? Donna Dalrymple.'

His mouth tightened. 'And she was Carmen Dalrymple. Do you still insist you're no relation—that you've never heard of her?'

'Yes, I do,' she returned quietly. The information had shaken her. Carmen was another relative to be found? Perhaps Beryl would know who and where she was.

His voice gritted as it cut into her thoughts. 'You also insist she had no hand in sending you here?'

'You're obsessed with this mad idea, Mr Armitage. Why on earth would anyone send me here?'

'To spy out the land, of course. She'll want to know if I've become involved with another woman. She *might* want to know how Jodie is faring, although that I doubt.' His voice had become harsh.

Donna almost choked with exasperation. She laid down her fork as she exclaimed in clear ringing tones, 'Mr Armitage, this conversation really frustrates me. Would you be good enough to tell me who on earth is Carmen?'

The dark brows rose as he regarded her. 'Didn't Beryl

tell you about her?'

'No. Why should she?'

'You're saying you don't know she's my ex-wife?'

She gaped at him. Her mouth opened but no sound came, then, swallowing, she said huskily, 'It would appear that I've been completely stupid. I suppose I should have guessed, but your—your marital situation hasn't really been laid before me. I presume you are divorced?'

'A year ago—after at least a couple of years of separation.'

'That's not very long. So what's bugging you? Why should Carmen send me to—er—spy out the land?'

'Because she wants to come back to me.'

'How do you know? Has she said so?'

'More or less. I had a letter two days ago. Apparently the marriage to Oliver Sloane has turned sour and, following hard on the letter, you arrive. It seems too much of a coincidence to me.'

She stood up and began to place the dishes on a tray. 'I can see it's useless trying to convince you,' she declared impatiently, 'especially when you're so boiled up with hatred against Carmen.' She paused to look at him thoughtfully. 'I suppose you realise that the sages say hatred is akin to love? If Carmen sets foot in this place you'll probably begin your marriage all over again.'

'*Never!*' he snarled furiously.

'Ah—that's what *you* say,' she jeered. 'Why don't you give it a chance and see what happens? Think how nice it would be for Jodie to have her mother home again.' She banged the last dish on to the tray and carried it out to the kitchen.

'It might be an interesting experience,' he admitted, following her and leaning against the bench while she rinsed the plates under running water. 'The only trouble is, I'm afraid poor Jodie might wake up with a jolt.'

She paused to look at him. 'What do you mean?'

'Carmen is not over-endowed with the maternal instinct, otherwise she would never have deserted the child.'

*'Deserted!'* Donna was shocked. 'I—I can hardly believe that any mother would do anything so—so despicable.'

He looked at her steadily. 'Can't you? The child is with me, isn't she? Why wasn't she taken with her mother?'

'Perhaps she meant to return to collect her.'

'Then why hasn't she done so?'

'I don't know.' The words came weakly.

'Perhaps I can enlighten you,' he said tightly. 'Carmen has never been madly fond of children, and it seems as if she's taken care not to become burdened by another child from this second marriage.'

For some reason unknown to herself Donna rose to Carmen's defence. 'Perhaps her maternal instinct has been slow to develop. I've heard it's quite late with some women.'

He gave a short laugh as his voice became heavy with sarcasm. 'You're suggesting it's now had a tardy blossoming?'

'I—I suppose it's possible——'

He took a deep breath. 'I'm afraid the situation is much more complicated than you realise, Miss Dalrymple. Not that I have any intention of discussing it with you.'

'No, of course not. I don't expect you to——'

He glowered at her darkly for several moments then appeared to have changed his mind, surprising her as he admitted, 'Would you believe that Jodie's red hair *niggles* at me?'

She was amazed. 'Niggles? I don't understand. What are you saying?'

He was silent for a short time before he continued in a low voice, 'All the members of my family have very dark hair, therefore I consider that my child should have hair much darker than Jodie's.'

'Perhaps her mother's hair was once that colour,' Donna suggested as she recalled her own red hair at Jodie's age.

'I doubt it. Carmen's hair is very like your own.'

She laughed. 'Mine wasn't always this colour. However—"convince a man against his will, he's of the same opinion still",' she quoted.

'Is that a fact,' he gritted, his jaw tightening. 'Perhaps you'd be interested to learn that I've been told Oliver Sloane has flaming red hair—and what's more, I strongly suspect that Jodie's will remain exactly like his!'

# CHAPTER THREE

DONNA stared at him speechlessly as the full meaning of his words registered with her, and then her voice came as little more than a whisper. 'Are you saying that Jodie is *not* your child?'

He paced the kitchen restlessly. 'I'll admit I've wondered about it. Every time I see the sun shining on that bright hair I'm reminded of Sloane. Nor is it a subject I'm in the habit of discussing, and how you managed to drag it out of me I'll never know.'

She wiped down the bench. As she did so she became thoughtful, and when they returned to the living-room she faced him squarely, speaking with frankness. 'It's possible you're being hasty, Mr Armitage. You could be jumping to the wrong conclusion, but no doubt it's your nature to make snap decisions and then refuse to change your mind.'

The dark grey eyes glinted at her. 'What the devil would you know about my nature?'

She forced herself to smile sweetly. 'You're forgetting I've already experienced your snap decision concerning myself,' she reminded him. 'You're so sure I'm related to Carmen and that she sent me to spy out the land. Huh! Of all the utter *rubbish*——'

He moved to stand closer, and as he stared down into her face he murmured, 'It's difficult to believe you're not related to her. When I look into your hazel eyes and at your auburn hair I see Carmen.'

She returned his gaze steadily as she asked, 'Would it surprise you to learn that my hair wasn't always this colour? When I was Jodie's age it was exactly the same as hers. At school I suffered from being known as Carrots— or Ginger.'

His expression became sardonic. 'Really? I suppose you expect me to believe that humbug?'

She flushed angrily. 'Are you accusing me of lying? Don't you realise that many people have hair that grows darker as they get older? Or are you too obsessed by your snap decisions and closed mind to even consider that fact?'

His quick intake of breath betrayed the agitation in his mind. 'I'm afraid there's more to it than that,' he gritted furiously, then strode to the side window where he stood staring out into a darkness that was now broken by a pathway of moonlight on the lake.

Something about the droop of his shoulders caused her to move to stand beside him, and, placing a hand on his arm she said quietly, 'Please believe me when I say I've no wish to pry——'

'So, what——?'

'And I know you declared you had no intention of discussing this matter with me, but to do so might help your peace of mind.'

'Are you suggesting I should visit a head-shrinker?'

She shrugged. 'It seems obvious to me that, deep down, something is bugging you. It could help to give it an airing. However, please yourself. While you're thinking about it I'll see if Jodie's asleep and well covered.'

In the bedroom she stood looking down at the little girl who lay with closed eyes. Was she Grant Armitage's daughter? Children had no say in the matter of choosing their parents, she realised.

When she left her bedroom she delayed her return to the living-room by making her way to the kitchen, where she examined the food stores for breakfast. But there was no need for concern because the cupboards and fridge were well stocked with such necessities as bread and butter, bacon, eggs, milk and cereals. Then, unable to find further excuse for her absence, she returned to the living-room.

He was sitting in the wing chair he had occupied earlier, his long legs stretched before him, his firm chin almost resting on his chest. The attitude made him appear to be deep in thought, but he looked up as she entered the room. Nodding towards the rocking-chair he said, 'Sit down. I've decided to put you in the picture.'

It was an effort to appear casual and to keep her curiosity in check. 'Are you quite sure you wish to confide in me?' she asked, looking at him doubtfully.

His voice sounded weary. 'To be honest I'd prefer to remain silent about the whole rotten affair. However, I suppose experience is dearly bought,' he added bitterly.

She said nothing as she waited for him to become launched into the story—whatever it was—but he seemed reluctant to begin. Instead he gazed across the water to where small lights twinkled in the darkness of the far side of the lake.

At last she said, 'I'll quite understand if you'd rather change your mind——'

He shook his head. 'I've no intention of doing that. If Carmen arrives—as I fear she will—it would be wiser for you to know the true situation. You can be sure she'll try to get you out and on your way.'

'Despite measles?' she asked.

'Yes. Jodie's misfortune might be something in our favour.'

'*Our* favour? I'm afraid I don't understand.' She looked at him wonderingly, sensing he had something in mind.

'The moment she knows Jodie has measles she's more than likely to back off—but only for a short period, of course, because as soon as she knows there's no need for her to give a helping hand, her cases will be carried upstairs. And that's where you can give assistance to me—if you will.'

She sent him a direct stare. 'In what way can I help, Mr Armitage?' she asked carefully.

'You can begin by being a little less antagonistic towards me——'

A laugh escaped her. 'You don't say! Hark at who's talking——'

He went on unperturbed. 'And you can make an effort to call me Grant instead of this continual Mr Armitage.'

'Well, that might be possible,' she conceded.

'You could also, upon occasions, even show a little affection. Let her imagine there's more between us than actually exists.'

She looked at him speechlessly until she found the words to say, 'What do you think that would achieve?'

'I'm hoping it will discourage her from thinking she can move in on a more permanent basis. If she has definitely left Sloane that is what she'll have in mind.'

Donna was aghast. 'Are you suggesting I should give her the impression that—that—we're *lovers*?'

'That's the general idea,' he admitted nonchalantly.

'You've got to be joking!' she snapped.

'Is the idea so very abhorrent to you?' he asked smoothly.

But she could only stare at him wordlessly as she tried to sort out the jumbled thoughts whirling about in her mind, most of them leaping towards indignation. *Pretend they were lovers?* How *dared* he have the temerity to make such a suggestion?

At the same time she became conscious of thoughts veering in another direction, thoughts causing her to recognise the passion lurking within the depths of this man. As a lover he would not be found lacking, instinct told her, and suddenly she was shocked to discover her sympathies were being drawn towards him.

'Well, what do you say?' he demanded impatiently.

'I think you've got a colossal nerve,' she retorted icily. 'And what's more—you must think I'm an idiot.'

He shrugged then gritted, 'OK, forget it. It was just that I had the mistaken idea you'd be willing to help.'

It was the word help that swayed Donna. That's why

she had stayed, wasn't it? To help. Normally it was her nature to help wherever she could, and now the accusation caught her on the raw. She looked at him doubtfully. Perhaps he wouldn't expect too much.

'What makes you so sure that Carmen will arrive?' she asked at last. After all, her assistance might prove to be unnecessary.

'Let's call it male logic,' he smiled.

'Oh, yes?' Her delicately arched brows rose a fraction as she regarded him. 'Is it that same male logic that told you I'd been sent to spy out the land? If so, it's not to be relied upon.'

'I'll show you her letter. Perhaps your female intuition can come up with a different answer.'

She was about to say she had no wish to read Carmen's letter, but, without further discussion, he rose from his chair and strode towards the desk at the far end of the room. And even when he tossed it into her lap she still felt reluctant to peruse the bold handwriting on the expensive gold-edged notepaper.

His mouth gave a wry twist as he observed it. 'Carmen loves gold,' he explained. 'Both in the pocket and out of it.'

'You sound very bitter.'

'Annoyed, rather than bitter, but more with myself than with her. It infuriates me to realise I was such an idiot, and to know that she imagines I'm still that same blind fool.'

She forced a smile. 'You've now hardened yourself against all women?'

'You can say that again.'

'I trust this anti-female attitude excludes little Jodie?'

'Of course it does. Just read the letter,' he snapped.

Her eyes scanned the page. 'Darling Grant,' it began. 'It seems so long since I saw you and our dearest little Jodie. In spite of everything that has happened I miss you both very much, and there are times when I long for the sight of your faces. I've tried to explain this to Oliver but he can't or won't understand.'

Donna raised her eyes to his face. 'She mentions Oliver.'

'She left me to go away with him.'

'Oh!' She returned to the letter. 'I know I've been a foolish woman, and you'll think I'm even more stupid when I say that at times the yearning inside me is almost too great to bear. How is my darling little Jodie? Do you help her with her school homework, or perhaps she's still too young for homework? Do you read to her, or does some other person read to her? I can't help wondering about this question. Has somebody else filled my place in your heart? You might say it is no longer my business, but I have to know these things and in some way I shall find out.'

Donna paused again to look at him. 'Now I can understand why you thought I'd been sent to—to spy out the land.'

'Read on,' he ordered tersely.

She turned to the letter once more. 'Life with Oliver is no longer the same,' it continued. 'At first we were so happy but now he seems to be angry with me most of the time and I can't help wondering why I was ever silly enough to leave your side. At least you never threw a wobbly just because I spent a little money.'

Staring at the page, Donna was unable to resist a question. 'Carmen is good at spending money?'

'An expert. She's probably running him into debt. It's also possible he hasn't as much money as she'd imagined——'

Again she raised her eyes to his face, this time noting the grim lines about his mouth. 'She says she can't help wondering why she ever left your side. Tell me honestly, why did she leave you?'

'Because she was in love with Sloane, of course. She had always been in love with him, even before she met me.'

'In that case, why did she marry you?'

He frowned, then sighed. 'I suppose you'd better hear the story from the beginning. Carmen's father is an accountant in Hamilton. Sloane joined him in the practice about ten years ago, and Carmen worked as their receptionist. Sloane took her out on numerous occasions and she fell in love with him. Eventually they had a quarrel, so she took a month's vacation and came to Beryl for consolation. And that's when I met her.'

'Why would she come to Beryl?'

'Because Beryl is a relative of some sort—a fact which also ties you to her in some way.' He paused, then admitted reluctantly, 'At the time I was young and vulnerable, and soon imagined myself to be in love with her.'

'You knew about Oliver Sloane?'

'Not at that time. In fact, not until after we were married did she mention his name. Inwardly, I suspect, she was fretting for him.'

'Yet she married you——'

'There was a very good reason. It seems that when she returned home they made up their quarrel and all went well for several months until, unexpectedly, Sloane made arrangements to take a position with a firm of accountants in London. He flew off into the blue from the Auckland International Airport without any suggestion of marriage to Carmen, nor even the slightest hint of taking her with him. She realised she'd lost him, so she came back to Taupo—and to me. We were married as soon as it could be arranged. Jodie was born seven months later.'

'Ah—she was a premature baby?'

'According to Carmen she was premature, but according to Doc Fraser she was a full term baby. Jodie was born in Hamilton and, because of our association, Doc Fraser was interested in my child——'

The awkward silence that followed his last words was broken by Donna. 'Did you ever meet Oliver Sloane?' she asked.

'No, but I'm told he's a tall, handsome fellow—with red hair.'

'Oh.' She was sorry she'd asked the question. It could only add coals to the fires of bitter recollections simmering in his mind.

He went on, 'Jodie was three when Sloane left England and joined a firm in Sydney. He contacted Carmen and arranged to meet her in Auckland.'

'It would be easy for him to fly across the Tasman Sea,' Donna said.

'And easy for her to visit friends in Auckland,' Grant added. 'Apparently he convinced her that she was the only woman he'd ever loved because, after one particular weekend, she didn't arrive home. She had returned to Sydney with him, and so far she hasn't been back.'

'Are you saying she just went away and left her child?' Donna asked in hushed tones. 'How could she do that?'

'I suppose it's easy enough for a woman whose maternal instinct is somewhat dead.' He frowned as he added thoughtfully, 'I don't mind admitting that this letter came as a shock.'

The story of Carmen had also been a shock to Donna. She had come to the North Island to find family, but she hadn't bargained on discovering a relative of Carmen's calibre—somebody who would desert her own child. And if Carmen was related to Beryl, it meant she would also be a connection of some sort to herself. Distant, no doubt—and the more distant the better, Donna decided.

She glanced down at the letter, then raised startled eyes to his.

'This is written from an Auckland address. It must mean she's already in New Zealand. It could also mean that she'll arrive soon.'

'That's right. And what is more, the divorce gave her access to see the child, if she bothered to care about exercising that right. So, will you do it?'

'Do what exactly?' she hedged.

'Let her see there's something between us, of course.

Comply with whatever opportunity offers. It might be a casual embrace, or something more telling.'

'It would be easier if I knew how far you expect me to go with this farce. It's all so—so indefinite.'

'Are you telling me you'd rather not play along with the idea?'

'Yes—most definitely, I am. I don't like it at all.'

'Why, for Pete's sake? It's not going to hurt you.'

'Because it's so dishonest,' she flashed at him. 'I hate dishonesty, and this is nothing more or less than a downright lie. You have no feeling for me apart from suspicion and dislike which—until the last half hour or so—you've made no attempt to conceal.'

'Perhaps I was rather hasty——'

'More than hasty,' she cut in.

'Am I to understand that you refuse to help me in any way at all?'

'I didn't say that. I suggest we play it by ear, as the saying goes. Wait and see what happens.'

'OK. I'll be grateful for that much, at least. In the meantime, we'll leave it at that.'

But Donna's own mind refused to leave it at that, and, watching him, she found herself wondering about the feel of his arms encircling her body to hold her against his broad chest. No doubt he'd kiss her with Carmen watching him, and as her eyes strayed towards his well shaped mouth with its hint of sensuousness, an unbidden thought sprang to her mind. *It would be nice to be kissed by this man.*

She turned away, fearing the possibility of those penetrating, dark-grey eyes reading her mind, and this almost seemed to have happened when he spoke in a surprisingly gentle tone.

'I can assure you it won't be so very unpleasant. I presume you've been embraced by a man before today?'

Her chin rose as she exclaimed indignantly. 'Of course I've had boyfriends—lots of them.'

'But not actual lovers,' he said quietly.

She tossed her head, then demanded coldly. 'How can you be so sure about that, Mr Armitage?'

'Because there's something about you—a sort of virginal look that suggests you're still—untouched. Am I right?'

'Mind your own business,' she flared in a fury.

'Ah, I thought so,' he returned drily.

She looked at him in silence, knowing he had guessed correctly. Now he'd be sure to think she was a stupid prudish miss—but after all, what did she care about his opinion of her?

His next question came abruptly. 'How old are you?'

'I'm twenty-two—just turned.'

'Carmen was twenty-two when I first met her. When I first saw you, there was one mad moment when I imagined the clock had been turned back.' His eyes half closed, he looked at her broodingly as though viewing a scene from the past.

It was enough to make her wince. 'So that when you kiss me you'll imagine you're kissing Carmen all over again,' she said sharply, aware that the thought irritated her. Then, telling herself not to be a fool, and in a voice that was full of understanding she added, 'You must have loved her very much.'

He shook his head. 'You're wrong. I know now that I only thought I loved her. I was infatuated. I'd had very little female company because my time had been spent studying to pass law exams, or out on the lake fishing with Dad and old Aubrey. My mother had died and I felt Dad needed my company.'

She nodded. 'I understand.'

'When I met Carmen I was like a monk emerging from a monastery. In fact Dad was beginning to feel worried about me. He was delighted when he saw me go overboard for Carmen.'

'Is your father still living?'

'Yes. He's the head of the firm. He lives in Taupo.'

She was thoughtful for several moments before she

drew him back to the former subject. 'There's still something you're forgetting. I doubt that Carmen will be fooled by any phoney embraces you see fit to bestow on me. She's sure to twig your insincerity. It'll stick out like a flag-pole.'

A smile lit his face, crinkling lines at the outer corners of his eyes. 'I'm glad you mentioned that point. It means we'll have to make it look real. I think I can be relied upon to do my bit—so it will only remain for you to respond to me.'

'Will it, indeed?' She stood up abruptly, feeling she'd left herself open to that suggestion. Then, glancing at her watch she added, 'If you'll excuse me I think I'll go to bed. I've had quite a day, driving from Auckland and—and everything else——'

He rose to his feet with a lithe movement and placed his hands upon her shoulders. Looking down into her face he said gravely, 'Very well, but before you go I think you could do with a little practice.'

She drew a startled breath. 'Wh-what do you mean?'

'When I kiss you under Carmen's gaze I don't want you to bounce away like a frightened rabbit. That would give the show away at once, therefore a little preparation would be wise—just something to enable you to become used to the idea of an embrace from me.'

'You seem to be so sure that the occasion really will arise.'

'Knowing Carmen, I'm positive you can put a ring round it. But, apart from anything else, I'd like to kiss you from sheer gratitude.'

'You're being hasty. I haven't promised anything definite yet.'

'I'm referring to the fact that you've put yourself out to take care of a child who's a stranger to you. I'd like you to know I'm grateful.'

'It's really Beryl I'm helping,' she pointed out, making a feeble effort to draw back from him, but the action only caused his grip on her shoulders to tighten as he stepped closer to her.

'I'm grateful for that, also,' he said in a low voice as his arms encircled her body to hold her against his muscular chest.

To cover her shyness she said, 'You're forgetting that to Beryl I'm a newly found part of the family—and family is something to be relied upon. Families share things, and that includes problems.'

'So it's really an overrated sense of duty,' he said with a touch of mockery.

'Not entirely. Jodie's a dear little girl. It's not difficult to hold out a helping hand where she's concerned.

He gave a short laugh. 'I'm warning you, Jodie can be a young madam when it suits her. There are times when a swift one on the backside wouldn't go amiss. Well, as I said before, I'm grateful for what you're doing for both Beryl and Jodie.' His last words had become little more than a murmur as one hand pressed her head against his shoulder.

His touch sent her pulses leaping, plucking at nerves and sending strange little tingles through her veins. Her cheeks felt hot as they rested against the smoothness of his suit jacket, and then unaccountably, her heart began to pound. *Keep cool, you fool*, she told herself. This is only a practice run. It means nothing at all. She also knew he was right to fear that an unexpected embrace would send her leaping away like a startled doe.

She felt his hand move to tilt her chin, and, unable to look at him, she closed her eyes. The gentle pressure of his mouth on her brow was strangely soothing, calming her jittery nerves as it wandered to reach her cheekbones, and causing her lips to part as they waited to meet his own.

There was nothing passionate or sensual about the kiss, nor were there demands for a closer encounter of a more intimate nature. However, she noticed that his hands slid down her body, kneading the muscles of her back as they pressed her against his lean form.

At last he released her, and as he stared down into her face he murmured, 'There now—that wasn't so difficult—was it?'

She shook her head, still unable to look at him.

'Good.' His tone became brisk. 'I hoped it wouldn't disturb you too much and that a kiss from me would have no emotional effect on you whatever.'

*'None whatever,'* she snapped vehemently, realising that he was warning her not to get any false ideas about its meaning.

'Excellent.' Her reply seemed to satisfy him. 'However, you'll have to do better with your response. Would it be possible for you to put your arms around me, or is that too much to ask? It would make it look much more convincing. Let's try again.'

*'Again?* Surely that's not necessary?'

'Of course it's necessary. "Practice makes perfect," as the saying goes——'

Before she could utter further protests his mouth had descended upon her own, but this time there was a difference in the kiss, for it was infinitely more sensual and held a depth that sent out an unspoken message. And, despite any intention she had to the contrary, her arms crept about his neck, clinging with an eagerness that made her wonder what she was doing. Again her lips parted as she responded to his kiss, and suddenly she knew she liked being in his arms.

But it was short-lived because he released her abruptly, almost thrusting her from him, yet at the same time he said with a hint of satisfaction. 'That's more like it. Lesson number one has gone quite well, I think. Now we'll have a cup of coffee, and with luck you'll find some of Beryl's shortbread in the cookie jar—that's if young Jodie hasn't already discovered it, of course.'

His manner of putting her from him had smacked of rejection while his words had hit her ears with the sting of a snub. It needed only his cool tone to tell her that her response had been more than he'd expected, and if she had any ideas of something deeper emerging from these moments she could forget it.

Mortified, she realised that his suggestion of coffee was meant to drag her feet back to earth from whichever cloud of hope she'd been basking on, and, seething inwardly, her hazel eyes flashed angrily as she said, 'I'm sure you're more than capable of making coffee for yourself. I'll see if Jodie's all right, and then I'm going to bed. Good night.'

As she walked away from him the feel of his gaze seemed to pierce her back, but she did not glance over her shoulder until she was in the passage and about to enter Jodie's room. By that time he had moved to the window and appeared to be staring out into the darkness, the hunch of his shoulder indicating gloomy thoughts.

She found the child sleeping peacefully, although it was necessary to remove Lulu, who was taking up most of the pillow and causing Jodie's small shoulders to become uncovered.

Jodie woke as Donna adjusted the bedclothes. 'I wanna go to the loo——' she muttered drowsily, scrambling out of bed.

'It's all that orange drink,' Donna explained as she put a gown round Jodie and shepherded her across the passage.

On the way back to the bedroom they passed Grant who watched them with a frown creasing his brow.

Jodie's flushed face looked up at him. 'Donna took me to the loo,' she informed him.

Donna avoided his eyes and ignored the statement, and as she tucked the child into bed once more she hoped Jodie would be settled down for the night. She then went to her own room, hung a few clothes in the wardrobe and prepared for bed.

A pile of National Geographic magazines left in the room for the interest of guests caught her attention and, leaning against the pillows, she was engrossed in an article with illustrations showing the treasures of the Vatican City when she was startled by a tap on the door. She looked up nervously and said, 'Come in——'

Grant walked into the room. He carried a small tray on which were two mugs of coffee made with milk. 'I thought you might enjoy this,' he said, handing her a steaming mug made of fine white china.

She was surprised. 'Thank you, you're very kind——'

'Not as kind as you're being to young Jodie,' he declared briskly. 'It hit me when I saw you take her back to her bedroom.'

She examined the pattern of red strawberries and green leaves on the white mug, but could think of nothing to say.

He added. 'It made me realise how necessary it is to have someone here with her.'

'Well, you've no need to worry now that I'm here—I mean—at least for the present.'

'I've never had this sort of problem before. She's never been sick—at least not since her mother left.'

'The spots will be out in a few days and as soon as there's no fear of infection I'll be on my way—and out of *your* way. Perhaps you could then get someone to stay on a more permanent basis.'

'You have someone in mind?' he demanded suspiciously.

She was silent, again examining the pattern on the coffee mug. There were white strawberry blossoms as well, she noticed.

'Because if you're thinking of Carmen, you can forget it,' he informed her, his voice cold.

'Carmen is the child's mother,' she reminded him. 'Don't you realise that girls need their mothers?'

'What exactly are you suggesting?' His voice was still icy.

'I think—if she has really left Oliver Sloane—that you should give her a second chance.'

The dark brows drew together as his face became

thunderous. 'You mean, take her back? Are you suggesting we should get married again? You must be raving.'

'But it would unite Jodie with her mother, and you would have *family*.'

'Dammit girl, you've got family on the brain. Don't you know that the majority of families fight like wild dogs?'

'Not my family,' she declared with lofty pride.

'No? I wouldn't know about that. But from what you've told me, you yourself know precious little about your family.'

'You're right,' she admitted dolefully as his words struck home. 'It's really why I'm here—to learn a little about it.'

'Haven't your parents put you in line with the family history?'

She sighed as she sipped her coffee. 'They don't seem to be able to tell me anything. Mother was an only child whose parents died when she was young, and all Father says is that his side of the family drifted apart and lost touch with each other.'

'Perhaps it's just as well. After all, who knows what skeletons can be dug up? You might not *like* your family.'

'Of course I'll like my family.' She then looked at him as a thought struck her. 'Did Carmen ever tell you much about her family?'

He shook his head. 'Nothing, as far as background goes, nor did she ever discuss any of her relatives. I don't think she had many.'

'I'm hoping Beryl will be able to give me some information, but so far we've had little or no opportunity to talk.'

'And now you'll be confined to these particular barracks for a while. You'll be bored. What shall you do with yourself all day?'

'Well, tomorrow there's a letter to be written to Santa Claus,' she reminded him.

'Confound it—and then Carmen's arrival will seem like a direct answer from the old boy. What on earth put the idea into the child's head?'

Donna sent him a level glance. 'The deep desire for her mother, of course. At some time every child writes a letter to Santa. Who else could bring such a gift?'

He was silent, staring into his coffee mug.

'And don't forget that you are Jodie's own personal Santa Claus, although she hasn't yet discovered that fact. Some children take longer than others to learn his identity.'

He left the bedside and began to pace about the room until he paused abruptly to swing round and scowl at her. 'If you imagine I'm to be bullied into an intolerable situation, you're very much mistaken,' he snarled. 'I'm a free man and I intend to remain in that happy state.'

She forced herself to smile at him. 'You're not free at all. You have the responsibility of a child—or have you passed that particular chore over to Beryl?'

'You underrate my feelings for Jodie,' he growled.

'Then how about being a little more demonstrative?' she suggested again tempering the words with a smile.

He took the empty coffee mug from her. 'You're not thinking clearly,' he rasped. 'Can't you see that my love for the child has kept her with me? At any time during the last three years I could have taken Jodie across the Tasman and dumped her with her mother. But I didn't.'

She looked at him curiously. 'Why didn't you?'

'Because I couldn't be sure she'd get the same care and attention that she gets here. But I'm forgetting that you don't know Carmen, therefore you can't possibly see the picture.'

He began to leave the room, and as he reached the doorway she said softly, 'Goodnight, Grant. Thank you for the coffee.'

He paused to look back at her, his face grave. 'Goodnight, Donna. I hope you sleep well.'

But as she lay in the darkness, sleep eluded her and, as

her mind became filled with thoughts of the man who had just left the room, she began to revise her opinion of him. He was not as cold and hard as she had at first thought, she was forced to admit to herself. It was true that he could have returned Jodie to her mother, and, despite the fact that he suspected the child had been fathered by Oliver Sloane, he *did* have affection for her.

As for the man himself—there was no doubt that he was an arresting specimen of masculinity, guaranteed to draw second, third and fourth glances from every woman in a crowded room. Apart from an athletic body that breathed strength, he possessed an aura that reached out to envelop most of them in his own personal net.

Except, of course, there was no way in which she would allow herself to drift into it—even if his kisses had been pleasant. In fact, they had been more pleasant than any other kisses she had ever experienced. Now why was that? she wondered.

There had been Sam whose kisses had tasted of peppermints, and Rex who had breathed strong tobacco over her. There had been Gary whose clumsy advances had nauseated her, causing her to spring out of his car and rush indoors. There had also been others, but not one of the men who had taken her out had touched her emotionally—which was probably the reason she was still a virgin.

But this man was different, she realised. She had never met anyone quite like him. Thinking of him, an unconscious smile touched her lips as she recalled the pressure of his arms about her body, the feel of his lips on her own. The firmness of his clasp had given her an intangible sense of security and, as the memory of it filled her with a strange comfort, her eyes closed and she slept.

# CHAPTER FOUR

NEXT morning Donna was wakened at seven o'clock by the sound of Jodie's hoarse voice calling her name. She had slept later than she had intended and it took a few moments to realise where she was, but she sprang out of bed, snatched at her dressing-gown and went to the child's room.

Jodie was sitting up in bed, her face still flushed. She sneezed, then said, 'I'm writing to Santa today. You gotta help me cos I can't write much yet. We gotta have paper and pencil——'

'How about some breakfast first?' Donna suggested.

Jodie flung herself back against the pillows petulantly. 'Don't want breakfast—want to write a letter—*now—now—now*——' she shouted, then began to cough.

'Tantrums will get you nowhere,' Donna advised. She looked at the child thoughtfully then added, 'I think I'll have my shower and get dressed—and then I'll pack my bag and leave.'

Jodie began to weep. 'You said you'd help me to write a letter,' she wailed. 'You *promised*——'

'And so I shall, as soon as you've eaten your cereal and milk.'

She left Jodie and made her way to the kitchen where she found that breakfast dishes had been left on the table. A quick survey of the rooms told her that Grant had already eaten and gone, and she wondered if he always left so early. She then recalled that he had to drive to the office in Taupo and was probably in the habit of making an early start.

A wave of disappointment swept her as she became aware that she had been looking forward to having breakfast with him, and then she called herself a fool because—obviously—he'd had no thought or desire to have breakfast with her. At the same time, the emptiness of the apartment was forced upon her, making her realise that without his presence the place was like a shell from which the life force had been removed.

Again, telling herself not to be idiotic, she showered and dressed, attended to Jodie and had her own scanty tea, toast and marmalade. She made her bed and tidied the living-room, then hesitated before entering Grant's room to make his bed. Would he think she was prying? she wondered.

But it was not her nature to tolerate a state of disorderliness, therefore, pushing aside the possibility of his suspicions, she entered the room and made the bed. As she straightened the blankets, the book he had been reading fell to the floor. She picked it up, glanced at it idly, then realised that the page had been marked by the letter Carmen had written. No doubt he'd taken it to bed to read it again—so did this mean he was having kinder and more forgiving thoughts towards his ex-wife?

Opening it quickly she refreshed her own memory concerning its contents, and, as her eyes travelled down the page, her attention was caught by Carmen's admission that at times the yearning inside her was almost too great to bear. Her yearning for her child—or for Grant? Donna wondered. Was it a letter that would affect and alter their lives? Perhaps Grant would consider he'd been alone in this wide double bed for too long.

No doubt Carmen's return would unite them as a family once more, but while family held a place of importance in Donna's mind the thought of Carmen lying naked beside Grant beneath the deep-gold cover gave her no satisfaction at all. In fact—strangely—it had a disturbing effect.

A husky voice calling from Jodie's room put an end to further wayward thoughts. 'Donna, when can I write my letter to Santa?'

'Right now, dear. I'll see if there's a pad and ballpoint pen on the desk.' Then, glancing at the letter in her hand she was startled to realise that in its own strange way this was also a letter to Santa Claus. It was Carmen's plea to come back, and the key to the situation was held by the Santa who owned Aubrey's Place. He would see the child's letter, and he would place it beside this one. How would he react?

'I know what I want to say,' Jodie stated with confidence as she sat up in bed. 'Will you do the writing part for me?'

'Very well. What do you want to say?'

'I'll say—I'll say you gotta bring my mother home to me.'

Donna smiled, then offered a word of advice. 'I don't think that's quite the right approach. Perhaps it would be better if you say Dear Santa Claus, will you *please* bring my mother home to me. You must never forget to say please and thank you. Santa considers it important for children to be polite.'

Jodie's eyes became round. 'Then I'd better say thank you to him for my Lulu doll. Santa brought her to me at Christmas time.'

Donna examined the beautiful doll with its flaxen curls and well made clothes. Only someone who cared for Jodie would have chosen one that was so expensive, and who else but the man himself? Despite the red hair that irritated him, and his suspicions concerning her paternity, he had endeavoured to give her joy on Christmas morning.

She found her thoughts warming towards him as she unthinkingly gave voice to her musing. 'Perhaps in his heart, your father would really like your mother to come home.'

Jodie looked up eagerly. 'Santa will want to know about that. Can you spell heart?'

'I think so,' Donna smiled, then sat on the side of the bed to draft out the letter Jodie wanted written. She printed it carefully, then handed the pad and pen to Jodie so that she could copy it. 'The letter must be in your handwriting,' she explained.

Jodie leaned over the pad, her pink tongue poking from the corner of her mouth. The effort did not take long because the letter was brief and to the point, and at last she leaned back against the pillow with a sigh of satisfaction. 'That's my bestest writing,' she announced as she handed the letter to Donna.

'It's very good,' Donna applauded, surprised by the neatness of the printed words.

A puzzled expression filled Jodie's eyes. 'How do we get it to Santa Claus? Do you know where he lives?'

'Something tells me your father will know,' Donna assured her with an inward smile.

'Yes, I suppose he will—he knows everything.' Jodie's face had become slightly more flushed, as though the effort of writing had tired her. Her eyes began to water and she coughed.

Donna made her lie down. 'Try and have a little sleep,' she advised, and, to her surprise, Jodie did not object to the suggestion. Her eyes closed and, with Lulu beside her, she was soon dozing.

Donna carried the letter to the window where she stood gazing thoughtfully across the wide expanse of water glistening beneath the morning sun. Below her, cars sped along the main highway towards the lake's southern end where the three mountains rose above their surrounding hilly land. Would one ever become weary of such a fascinating scene? she wondered. Perhaps, after a period, one would not even notice it.

She dragged her eyes from the panorama and read the child's letter again. 'Dear Santa Claus,' Jodie had printed in large lettering. 'Thank you for my Lulu doll. I love her. Would you please bring my mother home to me. In his heart, Daddy wants her to come home, too. Love from Jodie.'

What would be Grant's reaction to it? she wondered.

She carried it to the end of the long room and placed it on his writing desk, and as she did so Beryl's voice called to her from the bottom of the stairs. She went out to the landing and looked down upon an anxious, upturned face.

'How is Jodie this morning?' Beryl enquired.

'Just about the same,' Donna replied. 'If I didn't know better I'd say she was suffering from a bad bout of 'flu.'

'Kiri or Roy will bring you fresh food. Just ask if there's anything else you need.'

Donna sat down on the top step. 'At the moment my greatest need is information. Where does Carmen fit into the family?'

Beryl was startled. 'Carmen? You know about her?'

'Apparently we look alike.'

'Oh, he noticed it, did he?'

'I'll say he did. Nor was he amused. In fact, the sight of me gave him a real jolt,' Donna admitted.

'Did he really talk about her?'

'Quite a lot.'

'Did he actually tell you about—Oliver Sloane?'

'Yes. But I'm not really interested in Carmen's love life. What I want to know is how she *fits into the family*, and I've a strong feeling you can tell me. Can you spare a few minutes?'

'Oh yes, there's only one motel to do and Kiri's busy with that particular chore.'

'OK, so what can you tell me? Please, Beryl—I really want to know about the family. I mean about *our* family——'

Beryl sat on one of the lower steps and looked up at Donna. 'Don't you know anything at all about your own people?' she asked, her voice echoing her incredulity.

Donna shook her head. 'I know it sounds ridiculous.'

Beryl said, 'Well, it's like this—you and Carmen share the same great-grandfather. She's a little older than you, and was probably more similar to you when she was your age. That would have been when Grant first met her.'

'He said he met her through you.'

'Yes. I'm afraid he did—and I can understand the sight of you giving him a shock. It must have been like meeting Carmen again for the first time.'

Donna hesitated then asked, 'Did he love her very much? I mean, was he crazy about her?' She had no idea why this question should cross her mind or why the answer to it should be important. She only knew that it was and that it was something she had to know.

'It's strange you should ask,' Beryl said reminiscently. 'It's a question that I myself have often wondered about. At the time, he was young. I consider he was emotionally immature because he'd spent little time with girls. I always felt he went overboard too quickly and without knowing what love was all about.'

Donna laughed. 'Overboard? That's the word he himself used.'

'He did?' Beryl's upturned face betrayed surprise. 'It sounds as though he became very confidential. How on earth did you drag that piece of information out of him?'

'I don't know. He just told me. Incidentally, did you know he's had a letter from Carmen?'

Beryl's jaw sagged. 'I didn't. What does she want? You can be sure it'll be something for herself.'

'She doesn't sound very happy. In fact, he's half expecting her to arrive here.'

'Heaven forbid,' Beryl exclaimed, then added in horrified tones, 'I wonder if she's the C Sloane who's booked in for Easter. The reservation was made through a travel agency. Of course, you can see why she'd come at Easter.'

Donna looked blank. 'No, I'm afraid I can't see.'

'It's because the law offices close for quite a spell at that period,' Beryl explained. 'They have the long weekend as well as the following week. She'll expect Grant to be home, and she'll want to spend the time with him. She'll get a shock when she finds you in his apartment.' She laughed as though the idea struck her as being extremely funny.

'Yes—well—let's forget about her. You were going to tell me about our family,' Donna reminded her.

Beryl controlled her mirth. 'Oh yes, the *family*.' Her blue eyes looked up at Donna curiously. 'It's a wonder your father hasn't told you about his uncles.'

'I hate to admit this, but I didn't know he had any. In fact, I've often wondered if Father even *knew* about his family. It just seemed that he didn't belong to one. That's why I'm so thankful to find you—someone who can fill me in with some details.'

'You mightn't like them,' Beryl warned.

'I'm ready to learn the worst,' Donna smiled, confident that there couldn't be anything really shameful about her own family.

'Very well,' Beryl said. 'I take it you've never heard of your great-grandfather old Silas Dalrymple?'

Donna shook her head. 'Never,' she declared firmly.

'You and Carmen are both descended from him through the male line, which has given you similar hereditary bone structure and colouring.'

'I have my father's colouring, Donna admitted.

'Of course you have. Red and auburn hair is often passed on by the males in a family. Well, old Silas had three sons and one daughter who was my mother. But your father, his cousin in Auckland and Carmen's father are descended from each of the three sons. Can you work that out?'

Donna nodded. 'Yes, that's clear enough.'

'I understand the trouble began after the death of old Silas.'

'I suppose you mean estate trouble?'

'Yes. Mother was always tight-lipped about it because she didn't have the details of what actually went on. Also, it made her own brothers appear to be dishonest.' Beryl fell silent, giving Donna time to digest this fact.

Donna looked down at her, waiting patiently to hear more. There were so many questions she longed to ask, but she decided it would be wiser to not interrupt the flow of Beryl's thoughts.

At last Beryl continued. 'Old Silas had a well established business in Auckland—a large general store that sold clothing for men and women, furniture, hardware, lovely china, and all household necessities. You name it, he sold it. The three sons attended to the management of the various departments while their father kept his finger on the pulse of the entire business.'

'You're saying he was the general watchdog over everything?'

'Perhaps not a very wise one but, to give him his due, he tried to be fair to his children. When his will was read it was discovered that the store had been left equally between the four of them, to be run by the three sons together in harmony—or so he hoped.'

Donna was surprised. 'Are you saying he didn't leave the eldest son in charge?'

'He did not, and this infuriated William who was the eldest. The second son, Aleck, then pointed out that their father had always maintained that he had more business acumen than the other two put together—therefore *he* should be in charge. As for the third son, George——'

'George was my grandfather,' Donna put in. 'At least I know that much, because his grave is in Dunedin.'

'Well, George declared that the other two needn't imagine they were going to lord it over *him*. And as for my mother—being a mere female, she had no say whatever.'

Donna frowned. What had Grant said about families fighting like wild dogs? No doubt he'd known about this all the time—no doubt he'd been secretly laughing at her.

'They were at each other's throats,' Beryl said. 'And so it went on until things became so bad they began to accuse each other of helping themselves to the stock—which meant they were stealing from each other.'

'It sounds like a case of united we stand, divided we fall,' Donna remarked sadly.

'Indeed it was. And then one night a dreadful thing happened. The store caught fire and everything was lost—the building—the stock—the lot. Fortunately there was insurance, and after the site had been sold the remaining assets were divided between William, Aleck, George and my mother.'

'I'll bet they all blamed each other.'

'They did that exactly. The three brothers then parted company and Mother said that as far as she knew they never made contact or spoke to each other again. Your father's cousin in Auckland is descended from William.'

'Which means that Carmen's grandfather was Aleck—the smart one?'

Beryl laughed. 'That's what Mother used to call him—Smart Aleck. But I'm not sure Carmen is so smart, otherwise she'd never have left a fine man like Grant for that lanky, red-headed coot——'

'I thought it was because she'd always loved him,' Donna remarked. Then, with the desire to learn more about Grant niggling at her, she said, 'Was there no obvious affection between them?'

'None that I ever saw,' Beryl declared flatly. 'And things became much worse after the episode of the house.'

'House? What house do you mean?'

'A palatial home in Taupo was put on the market because its owners were leaving the district. Carmen set her heart upon it and pleaded with Grant to sell this place and buy it. He told her she had to be joking—that old Aubrey would turn in his grave. Carmen put on a scene and shouted that he thought more of old Aubrey's memory than he did of her. Honestly, I could hear her down in the kitchen.'

Beryl paused as she recalled the incident, then she looked up at Donna and added. 'Not long after that, Oliver Sloane returned to take up where he'd left off with her.'

'Then you weren't surprised when she left?'

'Not at all. But I was shocked when she deserted her child. I did my best for the poor little girl but it wasn't enough. She cried and cried for her mother, and for a long time I expected Carmen to return to collect her—but it didn't happen. She was probably enjoying a bright life in Sydney and the little one would have clipped her wings.'

Donna told Beryl about the special request in the letter to Santa Claus. 'Do you think it'll soften Grant's attitude towards Carmen?' she asked, her voice betraying more anxiety that she realised.

Beryl sent her a sharp glance. 'Would it matter to you if it did?' she asked, tempering the question with a sly smile.

'Of course not,' Donna retorted. 'Why should it?'

'Why, indeed?' Beryl was now grinning openly.

'Please don't hint that I've fallen for him,' Donna said crossly. 'Good grief, I only met him last night——'

'Stranger things have happened,' Beryl reminded her placidly. 'Well, I'd better get on with the job. Give me a call if there's anything you need.' She rose to her feet and disappeared towards the kitchen.

But Beryl's words had filled Donna's mind with thoughts she found difficult to push aside, and coupled with them was the memory of Grant's lips upon her own while holding her against him with a strength that left her breathless. Look upon it as a bright spot in an otherwise dull existence, she told herself lightly. Don't allow the aura of this devastating male to seep into your system and throw you off balance. Now then, what can you do to fill in time until he returns? No—dash it—you couldn't care less whether or not he ever returns——

The last mental statement was a blatant lie and she knew it. However, there was little cause to worry about filling in time because Jodie saw to that particular problem by spending a restless afternoon. Her eyes were red and watery, her nose was troublesome, the cough persisted and she was continually thirsty.

At last the child dozed, and it was during this period that Donna realised she hadn't even looked outside the back door at the end of the passage. Impulsively, she opened it to find herself confronted by a flight of steps leading down to the large gravelled yard, and from the landing she was almost dazzled by the breathtaking beauty of the late sun shimmering on the massed reds, golds and bronzes of the autumn-clad trees.

Beneath the trees were flower beds as eye-catching as the trees, and at one of them Roy attended to a border of flaming salvia bonfire. He paused to straighten his back and send her a friendly grin. 'Hi there—everything under control?'

'Yes, thank you—at least, I think so.' She paused before adding wistfully, 'Would it be possible to have some of those flowers for the living-room?'

'Sure,' he responded amiably. 'What would you like?'

'Oh, some of those lovely yellow and bronze chrysanthemums—and a few spiky cactus dahlias—and perhaps some zinnias——'

'Right, you shall have them.'

She watched while his secateurs snipped at stems, then, coming down the steps to take the blooms from him she said, 'Thank you, Roy, they're beautiful. In fact, it's all so beautiful. The autumn colours are fantastic.'

'That's because old Aubrey planted the right trees and because Taupo has a high altitude,' he told her. 'The colder air gives good colour. I'm afraid the first heavy frosts will finish the flowers, so enjoy them while you can.'

Returning to the kitchen she searched for suitable containers, then spent an enjoyable time arranging the flowers. At last they were placed in positions that showed them to advantage, and she stood back to examine the arrangements with a critical eye. A few alterations were necessary before she felt satisfied, but eventually she admitted to herself that the difference they made to the room was almost unbelievable.

She then turned to preparing the evening meal. The kitchen radio played soft music while she stood at the bench slicing beans, and, deep in thought, she failed to notice Grant's arrival until his arms slid round her waist.

She gasped, then swung round to face him, a bean still in her hand. 'I—I didn't hear you come in——'

'I came up the back stairs because my garage is situated near the foot of them.' He held her against him, then kissed her gently, his firm mouth moving softly across her closed lids before finding their way to her lips. 'Just practising,' he murmured nonchalantly at last.

'Is that so?' she returned calmly, determined to take the embrace casually, and hoping he hadn't noticed the quickening of her breath or the thumping of her heart.

He stared down into her upturned face. Regarding her seriously, he said with a hint of reproof, 'You're not responding convincingly. Your arms should be round my neck—clinging rapturously.'

Her cheeks had become flushed. 'You make me feel nervous. Are you sure this is really necessary?'

'I'm dead certain about it.' He kissed her again, his lips edging from her mouth to nuzzle the lobe of her ear. At the same time, his hands moved down her spine to press her closer to his body, and with his lips against hers again he muttered, 'Do you always manage to look so darned attractive—even when doing kitchen chores?'

'Do you always creep up from behind to take people unawares?' she retaliated, brushing his compliment aside.

'Only when tempted by a soft neck peeping through auburn hair, and especially when it belongs to one who prepares a meal for me.'

'Ah—the way to a man's heart being through his stomach——' She stopped abruptly, regretting those particular words.

'Exactly. Can you cook fish?'

'*Fish*?' The question surprised her. He could hold her in his arms—he could kiss her and talk about *fish*? It

brought her down to earth with a thud. 'Of course I can
cook fish. Do you want some cooked *now*?'

'No—not at present, thank you.'

She was puzzled. 'Then why do you ask?'

'Just checking. Most people who live near the lake are
experts at cooking fish, either in the pan or in the oven. I
don't want Carmen to walk in and find you staring at a
trout as though you've never seen one before and have no
idea of what to do with it.'

'I'm afraid I don't see the point.'

'It would be a dead give-away. It would tell her at once
that you're not in the habit of cooking it for me. She
knows I enjoy trout, and I'm anxious for her to imagine
you're a permanent resident in this area of the
establishment.'

'You mean that you want her to think I've been here
for ages—that—that I'm living with you?' She gave a
sudden laugh. 'Surely you can't be so naïve.'

He frowned. 'What do you mean?'

'You're forgetting the child. Jodie would tell her at
once that I've only just arrived. Can't you hear the
conversation between them? "Has Donna been here for
long, dear? Oh no, Mummy, she came on Monday."
Apart from that, anyone can tell her I've been here for
only a short time.'

'Not if I give directions to the contrary.' He scowled.
'But at least you've promised to stay for a while.'

She looked at him searchingly. 'Can't you hear the rest
of the conversation? Jodie will say, "Please, Mummy,
will you stay and look after me? Tell Donna to go
away"—and that's what will happen.'

He was still scowling. 'It won't if you stick to your guns
and play your part.'

'You mean, if I continue to respond to your phoney
kisses. I'm beginning to wonder why I should take part at
all in your little game!'

She turned to the bench again, aware that her hands
were shaking and knowing exactly why she was allowing

herself to become involved in his deception. The man
appealed to her and it was useless to deny it. There was
something about him that seemed to reach out and grab
her—to shake her into an awareness of his masculinity.
She sensed his vitality, and suddenly she knew without a
shadow of doubt that she *wanted* to feel his arms holding
her close to him—she *enjoyed* his kisses, pretended or
otherwise.

It was a moment of realisation that made her glad to be
occupied in preparing the meal, so that she did not have
to look at him. But, while this false relationship might
deceive Carmen, there was no point in allowing it to fool
herself into believing anything would ever come of it.

He left the kitchen and went to Jodie's room, but
returned almost immediately. 'She's asleep. Has she been
any better today?'

Donna shook her head. 'She was very fretful this
afternoon, although this morning she was perky enough
to write a letter to Santa Claus. It's on your desk.'

He went to the living-room, then returned to the
kitchen again, the open letter in his hand. The dark
brows drawn together indicated that he was not really
amused. 'This bit about "in his heart Daddy wants her to
come home too——" those aren't Jodie's words. That's
your idea.'

'Well—I might have mentioned it.'

'Do you honestly believe it?'

'Yes, I think I do,' she murmured, concentrating upon
the task in hand and unable to look at him.

He crossed the room to swing her round to face him.
'Why, for Pete's sake?'

'Because you protest too much. I think you're more
anxious to convince yourself—rather than Carmen—
that you don't want her back, whereas, in your heart of
hearts, you *do*.'

'Utter rubbish. What makes you think anything so—
so *stupid*?'

'Common sense,' she flashed at him. 'You're divorced

from her, so that particular trauma is over and done with. But it seems to me that you're worrying about coming face to face with her, which means you're afraid you'll weaken—and *that* means you still want her.'

'*Balderdash!* Now let me tell you this—*you don't know Carmen*. If she's got her mind set on coming back here she'll move heaven and earth to do so—and that will mean you in particular.'

'Then I'll have to try and keep my footing——'

'You do that. I'll be most grateful.' Firm fingers tilted her chin while his lips brushed her own.

The action caused her pulses to race and a deep, hissing breath escaped her as she became more annoyed with herself than with him. Stepping away from him she said sharply, 'Do you imagine I'm being fooled? I know exactly why these—these simulated kisses are being showered upon me.'

A gleam of amusement flickered in the grey eyes. 'You do? Would it be too much to share the reason?'

'You know jolly well you're not kissing *me* at all,' she almost hissed at him. 'You're kissing Carmen—but without committing yourself and without fear of involvement.'

'By Jove, that's an interesting theory. Tell me more. Why, for instance, would I be doing that?'

'Because—because you're reaching back into the past, to days when you thought she loved you. You're trying to recapture something.'

His eyes narrowed slightly as he followed her meaning. 'I believe you have a weird idea I'm suffering from nostalgia caused by your likeness to Carmen. Is that what you're trying to say?'

'Yes, that's it exactly,' she told him vehemently. 'And there's another fact that's very clear in my mind——'

'There is? Then let's have it. I'm all ears,' he drawled.

Her eyes ran from head to foot down the length of his athletic body, returning to rest on his handsome features. 'It's obvious you have a dominant personality,' she informed him coolly. 'Anyone can see your character is too strong to be ruled by a woman. You don't need me to protect you from Carmen, but you do need me to make her jealous. So please don't think I'm completely blind to your tactics—Mr Armitage.'

He looked at her in silence for several moments before he said, 'Very smart, Miss Dalrymple. You appear to have it all worked out.'

'It's not very difficult,' she retorted.

'No? Then perhaps you can tell me *why* I should try to make her jealous? Unless I'm very much mistaken her letter indicates she *wants* to return to me.'

Donna sent him a level glance as she said accusingly, 'It could be that you want to punish her—to enjoy a small amount of revenge before you take her in your arms and say all is forgiven.'

He looked at her thoughtfully before remarking in a quiet tone, 'You seem to have it all worked out, yet for some reason I suspect that these deductions are annoying you. You've even become quite flushed, although it's not hot in here——'

Exasperated, her control was achieved only by an effort, although her chin rose slightly. 'I am not annoyed,' she lied. 'It's just that I don't want you to think you're *fooling* me. No, not for one moment have I been taken in.'

'That point has already been hammered home,' he gritted, then a short laugh escaped him as he added, 'It would also appear that you consider I have a sadistic streak.'

She shook her head. 'No—strangely, I don't——'

'Thank you for that much.' He paused for a few seconds before adding, 'Perhaps I can give you a couple of extra thoughts to ponder. Does it not occur to you that she might be coming to me for the sole purpose of making her own husband jealous? It's possible he's been neglectful—or his eyes may have wandered in other directions.'

She was startled. 'No, I hadn't thought of that.'

'Or perhaps she's been smitten by a delayed spasm of motherhood. The letter did mention Jodie—if you care to remember.'

'Yes, it did,' Donna recalled in a low voice as she realised that Carmen could have more than one reason for returning to Aubrey's Place. But the main question dominating her mind concerned Grant. What effect would the return of his ex-wife have upon him? Not that it held any particular interest for *her*. Donna assured herself with a strong degree of firmness.

It was almost a relief when the subject was changed by Jodie indicating her wakefulness by calling from the bedroom. 'Donna—Donna—I can smell vegies cooking,' she complained hoarsely. *'I won't eat vegies——'*

Donna went to the bedroom door. 'I'll give you only a little,' she promised. 'You must eat something to help you get better.'

*'I won't—I won't——'*

Grant joined Donna at the doorway. 'What's all this nonsense about not eating vegetables?'

Jodie sat up and stared at him. 'Daddy, did you bring me a present? I want a present——'

Grant grinned at Donna. 'Carmen's daughter, you understand.'

'It's just that she's not well,' Donna defended.

'You think so? When you know her thoroughly you'll learn that she's even more demanding when she *is* well.'

'If you expect me to be here long enough to know her thoroughly, I'm afraid you'll be disappointed—Mr Armitage.'

He looked at her steadily but said nothing.

Jodie's tearful voice then came from the bed. 'Daddy—Daddy—*I want a present——*'

'OK—so I did bring you a little something.'

'What is it? *Give it to me at once——*'

Donna was shocked by the child's manner. Fretfulness was one thing, but this rudeness was not to be tolerated, she decided as she watched Grant go to the living-room and return with a square flat parcel. Before he could give it to Jodie she laid a hand on his arm and said, 'Please, let me show it to her.'

Taking it from his hand she carried it to the bedside and spoke to the child. 'You see? Your father has brought you a present. Doesn't this show you he loves you very much?'

Jodie stretched out a hand. *'Give it to me,'* she shrieked huskily. 'I want it—I want it——'

Donna held the parcel aloft. 'You'll have it when you've had something to eat.'

*'No—no—I won't eat vegies——'* The flushed face was pressed into the pillow.

Donna compromised. 'Well, how about some nice custard and jelly?'

'All right.' The agreement came sulkily.

The custard made with milk and eggs, plus the jelly, disappeared in record time. Jodie then snatched at the parcel, tore off the wrapping and gazed entranced at the picture on the lid of a box containing a jigsaw puzzle. 'It's a doll's tea party,' she exclaimed joyfully. 'That one looks just like Lulu.'

'So what do you say?' Donna prompted gently.

Jodie looked at Donna and then at Grant. 'Thank you, Daddy,' she muttered after a few moments of thought.

Grant then drew Donna out to the kitchen where he kissed her. 'I could do with you around this place,' he told her seriously.

# CHAPTER FIVE

DONNA refused to allow his words to go to her head. Every man who had been left with the care of a child needed a woman about the house, and he'd merely been pointing out this fact to her. That's all there was to it. Nothing more.

But later, as they sat at their meal, Grant examined the flower arrangements with interest. 'You've made the room look attractive,' he remarked with undisguised appreciation. 'It hasn't looked like a real home for— three years at least.'

'I didn't pick them,' she assured him hastily. 'Roy gave them to me, although I'll admit I asked for them. I don't know when I've seen such fantastic colours standing against a blue sky. I mean the liquid ambers——'

'Aubrey planted them years ago, and now they make the lodge an autumn showplace. Did you know Roy worked for him?'

She was surprised. 'No—Beryl didn't tell me, but then I haven't been here long enough to know anything.'

'Roy and Beryl have been here for years. In fact, Roy brought Beryl here when they got married. He likes to keep the grounds in a state that would have pleased old Aubrey. If I, as present owner, dare to make a suggestion, his mind immediately questions whether it is something of which Aubrey would have approved.'

Donna laughed. 'Now that's what I call carrying loyalty to excess. I wish I'd known old Aubrey,' she added softly. 'What did he look like?'

'An aristocrat. A tall, commanding figure with white hair, an aquiline nose and twinkling blue eyes. His back was as straight as the proverbial ramrod.'

'He sound like an old soldier.'

'He was, but he preferred to be thought of as an old fisherman. My own father has always been a keen fisherman, but it was Aubrey who taught me all I know about trout fishing.'

'I suppose there's a lot to learn,' she said, encouraging him in what must be a favourite subject.

He nodded. 'Of course, one is always learning about the time factors—if you know what I mean.'

Donna shook her head. 'I'm afraid I'm quite ignorant about fishing.'

'It means what the trout will do at certain times of the day, such as when they rise to feed and what there is for them to eat. Aubrey taught me the art of dry fly-casting, and what to use at different times of the year. Sometimes there's a little brown beetle to which they're rather partial, and of course there are various types of flies.'

Grant's voice rang with enthusiasm as he became launched on other aspects of fishing, and she guessed that mentally he was away out on the lake with old Aubrey beside him. But suddenly he left the table to disappear into his room, then returned with a small metal case containing an assortment of imitation flies. Opening it carefully he said, 'These are used at various times of the day. They're all named. This is a Red Dragon and this is a Brown Owl. These are spinners, which flash in the water.'

She watched him touch the small feathered or metal scraps with gentle fingertips. 'These were Aubrey's flies?' she asked with sudden insight.

He nodded without speaking, and she guessed that the sight of them affected him emotionally. 'I don't use them—I just keep them,' he admitted, then went on to tell her about incidents concerning the big ones that had got away.

She enjoyed listening to the pleasant timbre of his deep voice, and, while giving him her rapt attention, she found she could study his attractive face without appearing to do so. Her eyes became riveted on the crease in his cheek, then strayed to his sensuous yet finely chiselled lips—lips that had so recently rested upon her own.

She dragged her mind from the memory, forcing herself to concentrate upon what he was saying about the difference between brown trout and rainbow trout, and the all-absorbing sport of catching the fish with a rod.

But was fishing the best hobby for him? she wondered. To her, it appeared to be a solitary pursuit that would enable bitter thoughts to rise and taunt his memories. Naturally they'd centre upon Carmen, and later he'd return to these rooms which would be empty except for Jodie, whose red hair could only add further stings to his recollections.

'Have you ever been out on Lake Taupo?'

The question cut into her thoughts. 'No, there's been no opportunity. It must be exhilarating,' she added wistfully.

'During my Easter break I'll take you out in the launch.'

'That's if I'm still here and if you have time to do so,' she smiled. The thought of being out on the lake with him was exciting.

'Still here? Are you saying you won't be here for the remainder of your vacation?' he drawled in a bantering tone.

'Of course I won't. Jodie's period of isolation won't last for ever—and then I'll be on my way.'

'Strange,' he mused. 'I'd begun to imagine you might remain here until it was time for you to return to your job in Auckland.'

'Had you, indeed?' She searched his grey eyes for a hint of seriousness to the lightly spoken words before she added, 'You're forgetting that I can be replaced here very easily. In fact I suspect the time is drawing near because Beryl told me she'd booked in a C Sloane for an indefinite period. She said she hadn't connected the name with Carmen.'

'You've been discussing her with Beryl?'

'I asked her to tell me about my own family and where Carmen came into it,' she explained casually, hoping he would not think their conversation had been dominated by the situation between Carmen and himself. 'Please remember that I came here to learn about my family.'

He grinned. 'I take it you weren't amused by the details Beryl presented?'

'I was not. In fact, I was really disappointed. I'd always thought of a family as being a unit against the world— relatives tied by blood who could be relied upon. They'd be loyal to each other and ready to hold out a helping hand.'

'I'm afraid the average family knows little about those high ideals,' Grant said grimly. 'They consist of very few people like yourself.'

'Like me?' She was startled by the suggestion.

'Well, you held out a helping hand, didn't you? Otherwise you wouldn't be here. Not everyone would allow a child with measles to mess up their entire vacation.'

'It was really to help Beryl——' she began.

'Rubbish,' he retorted curtly. 'It was much more than that. You saw you were needed and you stepped into the breach because it's your nature to do so.'

A faint smile touched her lips. 'Thank you for the compliment. It's nice to be appreciated.'

'I shall appreciate you even more when Carmen arrives,' he told her in a low voice.

'You mean when we—put on an act?'

His eyes held an amused glint. 'Will it be so very difficult for you to be held in my arms?'

Donna thought for a moment. 'I can assure you, it won't be easy.'

'I suspected as much. That's why I decided a small amount of practice would be wise.' He studied her face closely then asked, 'Why should you find it even remotely difficult?'

She flushed beneath his searching scrutiny. 'As it happens, I'm not in the habit of openly showing affection to a man—especially to a virtual stranger—and even more especially before the eyes of another person.'

'So, you're not in the habit of showing affection to a man. Does this mean you haven't a boyfriend? I can see you're not wearing a ring, but isn't there someone in particular who holds your interest—or your love?'

She shook her head. 'No, there's nobody——'

'In that case, kissing me won't make you feel guilty,' he declared with satisfaction. 'But even if there had been someone—a swain waiting impatiently for your return to Auckland—there'd be no need for concern because, as you yourself said, this is only an act.'

'That's right.' She nodded in agreement, yet for some strange reason found herself unable to look at him. *Only an act.* The words had a hollow ring that spoke of emptiness. Was he warning her to make sure she *kept* it as an act? Was she telling her that he himself had no intention of allowing their charade to progress beyond a stage performance?

She shook herself mentally. Was there something *different* she should be expecting from him? No, of course not. He had merely asked for her assistance in the situation with Carmen. That was if it arose—and he seemed to be sure that it would.

He said, 'I'm warning you that Carmen will be difficult to convince. If I simply *tell* her I'm interested in somebody else it won't mean a thing. She'll brush it aside and it'll hardly register with her. But if I can *show* her, it'll make all the difference. Do you understand?'

'Yes, I understand.' She left the table and went to the side window where she stood staring out into the darkness. 'And when it's over I can go home and forget the whole episode,' she remarked over her shoulder.

'You shouldn't find that too difficult to achieve,' he said quietly as he crossed the room to stand behind her, his hands slipping round her body.

His touch caused her to jump and take in a sharp breath. Colour rushed to her face as she gave an exclamation of protest and tried to sweep his hands away.

'Stop being so jittery,' he advised. 'Learn to take it in your stride. Try to remember we're endeavouring to fool one who's an expert in the art of fooling others.'

'You mean that you're trying to fool *her*—but I think you're moving too quickly. Carmen isn't here yet, nor do I intend to be rushed into the arms of a man I met only yesterday.'

'I see. You're asking me to put on the brake?'

She nodded. 'At least—keep it handy.'

'Very well. Let's have some coffee.' His hands dropped to his sides and he left her abruptly to stride towards the kitchen.

Unreasonably, his departure brought a surge of disappointment, and although she waited for him to take her in his arms again it didn't happen. The rest of the the evening was spent in casual but amiable conversation while she told him a little about life in Dunedin, and eventually she went to bed—unkissed.

Later, as she lay in her bed, she realised that *she* was the one who needed the brake. She was allowing uncontrolled thoughts of this man to dominate her mind. She was acting like an idiotic schoolgirl instead of the well adjusted and self-disciplined young woman she considered herself to be.

She closed her eyes, determined to go to sleep, but still the questions squirmed in her mind, writhing and tumbling over each other like a bowl of newly caught eels. Exactly how sincere was he in his desire to avoid further entanglement with Carmen? How vulnerable would he be when face to face with her? And what was he doing at this very moment? Was he reading—or sleeping—or lying in the darkness thinking of his ex-wife? Was he wondering how long it would be before she lay stretched beside him again?

But until that happened, Donna thought, his arms would continue to slip round her own body, causing her heart to skip beats and her spirits to soar towards a fool's paradise. Even now the memory of his arms around her caused an inner fluttering as she thought of what could follow. Yes, indeed, she was the one who needed the brake, common sense warned for the second time.

Therefore tomorrow would be different, she told herself firmly. Tomorrow—if he dared to put his ridiculous tactics into operation—would be when she'd give him short shrift. And, while trying to sort out ways of putting Grant Armitage in his place, she fell asleep.

The next day was Wednesday. The frosty morning dawned with the cloudless and pristine freshness of autumn and, although Donna reached the kitchen earlier than on the previous morning, she found that Grant had again already left for the office. Conscious of disappointment, she sighed and attended to Jodie, whose condition was similar to yesterday, although Donna imagined she detected a slight improvement.

The child was a little less fretful but perhaps this was because she'd become engrossed in the new jigsaw puzzle. Nevertheless it was a relief when, on hearing a knock on the back door, Donna opend it to discover Doc Fraser on the landing.

He gave her a brief nod. 'Good morning. I thought I'd take a peep at the wee lassie before going out on the lake. How has she been behaving?'

Donna told him all she could, then led him into the bedroom where he examined Jodie and took her temperature. 'It's running its usual course,' he said. 'The spots should be out tomorrow. Aye, by tomorrow afternoon she'll look a real sight. And then the isolation can end ten days after the first spots have appeared. In the meantime she must be kept in bed for at least a week.'

When he left she accompanied him out to the landing where he paused to look at her. 'Speaking of sights— you're a bonny sight yourself. Aye, you are that.'

She brushed the compliment away with a light laugh. 'Thank you—but look at that one over there.' A gesture indicated the trees where the massed reds and golds glistened brilliantly in the morning sun. 'Have you ever seen anything like it?'

He turned to stare at the kaleidoscope of autumn colour. 'Aye, it really is something. Just look at that crimson Virginia creeper covering Grant's garage. I was here when Aubrey planted it. Dear old Aubrey, how we miss him. It takes a long time to become used to a person's absence.' He sighed and went down the steps.

Watching him descend, Donna echoed his words in her mind. *A long time*. It had taken Grant a long time to become used to Carmen's absence—and now she was about to return to stir up old memories and perhaps creep back into his heart. That was if she'd ever really left it, which was something Donna was beginning to wonder about.

Depression began to seep into her soul until it held her in a grip that was difficult to shake off. The thought of Carmen's arrival gnawed at her mind, making her feel restless and ill at ease, until at last she took control of her emotions and told herself not to be a fool. The child's mother was coming to see her. That was all.

But deep within herself Donna suspected that that was not all. Carmen was really coming back to see Grant. She was returning to fling herself into his arms and into his bed. OK, so what did she care about that particular state of affairs? Not one iota—or so she assured herself.

Further, this man was still virtually a stranger, and that was another reason why he meant nothing to her. Yet somewhere at the back of her mind there was a niggling doubt about the truth of this assertion.

Nor could she find any reason for the constant glances at her watch, or for her own mental ticking off of the hours that would bring him home. And although she refused to admit it even to herself, she was not only waiting for his return with a subdued sense of excitement, but had already planned what she would prepare for the evening meal. Naturally it would be fish, just to prove she was capable of serving it as an attractive dish, and for this she would need parsley which was sure to be growing in the vegetable garden.

However, before she could go in search of it Jodie's voice called from the bedroom. 'Donna—Donna—come and help me——'

She hurried along the passage to find Jodie sitting up in bed with the jigsaw puzzle on a tray, and, looking at her critically, Donna decided that perhaps there was very little improvement in the child's condition as her catarrh was still troublesome.

'I can't find the pieces for Lulu's face,' Jodie complained tearfully.

'Perhaps they're on the floor.' Donna knelt to pick up the fallen pieces which she deftly put into place. 'There you are—now try and find all the bright yellow pieces that make her dress.'

'When will Daddy be home?' Jodie demanded.

'Oh, not until this evening, and that's hours away.' She didn't even have to look at her watch to judge how many hours.

'Will he bring me a present?'

'I doubt it. Didn't he bring you one last night?'

'Ring him on the phone,' Jodie commanded. 'Tell him to bring me another present.'

Donna was appalled. 'Certainly not. You haven't even dealt with this one yet.'

Jodie's flushed face showed temper, her voice rising to an angry squeak. 'You gotta ring my Daddy and tell him he's gotta bring me another pressy——'

Donna kept her patience under control with difficulty, and she was about to utter a sharp reprimand when, to her amazement, the phone rang. She hurried to the living-room, and even before lifting the receiver a sixth sense told her it would be Grant.

'Hello?'

His deep voice came over the line to send strange little tingles into her nerves. 'Donna, I'm afraid I had to miss having breakfast with you——'

'Do you always leave for work at the crack of dawn?'

'Only when there's a lot to be done in the office. Are you all right? Things aren't getting you down?'

'No, of course not.' His questions lifted her spirits. He was actually wondering whether or not she was all right. 'Why would you think anything was wrong?'

'I just wondered if anyone in particular had turned up yet.'

'No, not yet.' She knew he meant Carmen and her spirits sank back to normal as she realised he hadn't been worrying about her at all. He was merely ringing to check if his ex-wife had arrived. Did this mean he was dead keen to see her?

His voice came over the line again. 'How's the patient? Is she screaming for more pressies?'

She was amazed by his perception. 'How did you guess?'

'Have you forgotten I happen to know that young minx particularly well? Actually, I've bought her a few new books.'

'You spoil her atrociously.'

'Well, the kid's not well, and they'll help to keep her occupied over Easter.'

'You're forgetting that Santa Claus is about to drop by out of season with the biggest gift of all.'

'I hadn't forgotten.' The reply came quietly.

'That's why you *really* rang, isn't it? You were most anxious to know if she'd arrived——' Donna shut her mouth abruptly, furious with herself for having uttered those particular words.

'You're mistaken,' he drawled. 'I rang for an entirely different reason. It was to tell you I'll not be home for dinner this evening.'

'Oh!' She was swept by intense disappointment and she knew that if she said anything further her voice would betray the fact.

'It's the work in the office,' he explained patiently. 'There are several things I want to clear up before we close for the Easter break. Did you realise our office closes during the following week? It means I'll be home—but I think I mentioned it before——'

'Yes. Beryl also said something about it. That's why——' She fell silent, not wishing to pursue that subject.

'Yes? That's why——?' he prompted.

'Well, that's why Carmen has chosen to come at this particular time,' she responded coolly.

'You could be right about that,' he chuckled. 'Incidentally, it'll be late before I arrive home, so don't wait up for me.'

'Why should I do that?'

'Only to make me a nice hot drink. It's always better when someone else serves it.'

'Is it indeed? You've broken your arm or something?'

'Of course not——'

'Then you'll be able to make your own hot drink.' She paused, regretting that acid remark, then asked, 'I suppose you'll be away early in the morning—*again*?'

'Yes, but it can't possibly bother you. And I'll be working late tomorrow night—*again*. Goodbye.'

'Goodbye.' She replaced the handpiece with a feeling of dejection although she didn't dare ask herself why this should be.

However, the rest of the day passed rapidly because Jodie kept her busy with drinks and visits to the toilet. The child's mood became irritable and her face seemed to have become even more flushed than it had been. She complained about a sore mouth, and when Donna peered into it she detected the bluish-white spots that heralded the main rash that was due to break out on Jodie's face and body.

It began to appear late in the afternoon and consisted of groups of small dusky-red spots on her brow, cheeks,

chin, and behind her ears. By evening her temperature
had risen, her throat was sore and her catarrh was worse
than it had been during the day. The jigsaw was pushed
aside while Donna sat near the bed and read stories until
the child's even breathing told her that Jodie was asleep.
She then tiptoed from the room.

Her intention had been to get into bed and read but, as
she began to undress, her thoughts turned to Grant's wish
for a hot drink after his evening's work. At least she
could make him a plate of sandwiches, she decided,
therefore she slipped into her pink, floral dressing-gown,
fastened its line of front buttons and went to the kitchen.

Thinly cut slices from a wheatmeal loaf were soon
buttered, and she then opened a small tin of red salmon
imported all the way from Canada. A sheet of transpar-
ent cling-film was placed over the plate and, having
removed the empty tin and put away the bread and
butter, she left the kitchen.

But instead of going to bed she wandered into the
living-room where she stood at the side window to watch
the cars coming from the direction of Taupo. The time
was almost ten o'clock, and at this hour of the night there
was not so much traffic on the road, so perhaps the next
car would be his—or the next—but neither showed signs
of reducing speed.

Car after car sped past, and as Donna watched the
intense darkness being broken by the glare of their
sweeping headlights she asked herself why she was
standing there. *Go to bed, stupid,* she muttered fiercely,
yet the desire to see Grant was so strong it kept her glued
to the window.

Eventually a car came slowly and, as she watched it
turn on to the fishing lodge driveway, Donna's heart
began to beat a little faster. Was it Grant, or merely a late
arrival to the lodge? She hastened to the kitchen where
she peeped from the window to be rewarded by the sight
of red tail-lights glowing from the garage door.

Now I'll go to bed, she told herself firmly, but it

seemed that she lacked the power to do so. Instead, she was gripped by an inner excitement that had grown out of all proportion and, after lifting cups from their hooks, she filled the electric kettle.

She heard the creak of the stairs as he ascended them, and when the back door opened and closed she was unable to resist the temptation of going out into the passage to greet him. At the back of her mind she really expected to be taken into his arms—just for practice, of course—but it didn't happen.

Instead he stood regarding her with a hint of surprise, the parcel of Jodie's new books under his left arm, his briefcase swinging from his right hand. When he spoke his voice betrayed fatigue.

'You're still up. I thought you'd be in bed and dead to the world.'

She raked in her mind for an answer. 'I waited up to report on Jodie's condition. The poor child's been very cross this evening. The measles are reaching their peak; the first of the spots have arrived.'

The fact that she had waited up to see *him* was hardly to be admitted, even to herself, yet she knew this to be a fact. Then, brushing the thought aside, she went on hastily, 'When we spoke on the phone I forgot to tell you that Doc Fraser called this morning. He said we can expect Jodie to look a real sight tomorrow.'

He rubbed his chin thoughtfully. 'He did? Well, that should have interesting results.'

*'Interesting results?'* Not quite sure of his meaning she sent him a puzzled glance. 'Interesting is not the word I'd attach to Jodie's condition. Distressing or pitiful, perhaps, or something to indicate a feeling of sympathy for her.'

'You've failed to latch on to my meaning,' he said wearily and without bothering to explain himself. Instead he said, 'I understand the spots herald the beginning of the end.'

'Yes, although Doc Fraser reminded me that isolation

continues for ten days after the first spots appear.'

'*Ten days?*' His voice echoed concern. 'In that case I can't help feeling guilty about you.'

'About *me*?' I'm not afraid of catching measles. I've had them.'

'I'm referring to the fact that your holiday will have been completely ruined,' he said sharply. 'I had no idea it would take so long, nor do I like being under such an obligation——'

'Please don't worry about it,' she said swiftly. 'Perhaps I'll be able to take a break later in the year.'

'But that will be useless. It'll be winter, when the weather is most unsuitable.'

She smiled as though a bright thought had just struck her. 'Don't you think Carmen could relieve me when she arrives? I feel sure she'll be longing to take over the care of her own child.'

'You do?' Sardonic lines appeared about his mouth. 'That's what I meant when I said that the sight of Jodie's spotty face might have interesting results.'

'I don't understand——'

'Carmen's not the compassionate type. She's more than likely to back off in horror.'

'But—Jodie would be so distressed.'

'Yes. So what?'

'I can't believe that Carmen will turn away from her own child; especially when she's sick.'

'You're forgetting that she's already left her once. However, we'll just have to wait and see what happens.' A hard note crept into his voice. 'You're positive the spots have arrived?'

'Of course. Come and see for yourself.'

'No, I'll take your word for it. She might be disturbed and it's better to let her sleep. Now then, what about a hot drink?' He strode to the kitchen where the sight of the sandwiches made him pause. 'You made these for me?'

'Aren't you in need of something after an evening's

work?' She kept her tone light as she took a jug of milk from the fridge.

'Thank you, I appreciate your thoughtfulness.' He bent swiftly and brushed her cheek with his lips, almost causing her to spill the milk. Then, taking the jug from her, he placed it on the bench and kissed her again, this time with more purpose.

Determined to take it in her stride she was annoyed to notice a tremor in her voice as she tried to ask casually, 'What would you like? Cocoa—Horlicks—or coffee made with milk?'

'Coffee, thank you, with half milk and half water. You'll join me, I hope?'

She nodded, knowing that not even wild horses could drag her to bed at that moment. Besides, it would be impolite to leave him to have supper alone—at least, that's what she told herself.

The sandwiches and mugs of steaming coffee were placed on a tray which Grant carried into the living-room. He then moved the small table from the end of the room to beside the settee, indicating that she should sit next to him.

A small flutter of excitement took hold of her while she watched him enjoy the sandwiches, but she managed to keep it under control as she listened with interest while he recounted a little of the day's problems that had spilled over to keep him late at the office.

Without mentioning the names of clients, he spoke of the strange and unfair wills that various people had been set on making, and he also told her about two men who were neighbours, but who communicated with each other only through a solicitor. Finishing the last of his coffee, he turned to grin at her. 'Would you believe that the son of one has married the daughter of the other? The two fathers are now jumping up and down with rage.'

'So that both are now making new wills?' Donna smiled.

'I understand there's talk of it. The young couple asked

what I thought they should do about it. I pointed out there's very little they can do, although I advised the bride to become pregnant as soon as possible. There's nothing like a baby to bring grandparents running at the double.'

Donna laughed. 'You're very astute.'

'Am I? I sometimes wonder about it. By the way, you were waiting for me tonight.' It was a statement rather than a question.

She avoided his eyes. 'Was I? What makes you so sure?'

'The fact that I caught a glimpse of you standing at that side window over there. I don't believe you were counting the cars that raced past. Why not admit it?'

She raked in her mind for words that would not betray just how keen she had been to see him return home. 'Well, I did hope you wouldn't be too late,' she said at last.

'Why?' The question snapped abruptly. 'Have you become bored with this situation?'

She smiled as she thought of the trips to the toilet and bathroom. 'Oh no, poor little Jodie's state kept me too busy to be bored.'

He turned to face her, one arm resting along the back of the settee. 'If you were here alone, all day and every day, and without Jodie to keep you occupied, I fear you'd soon become bored and lonely.'

'Was loneliness Carmen's trouble?' she asked with a flash of intuition.

'I suppose it was—plus the fact she was married to the wrong man, or so she thought at the time.' His tone had become bitter.

Donna looked at him intently. 'But you feel sure she has now changed her mind?'

'It seems like it. So tell me, if you had been in Carmen's place what would you have done to combat boredom and loneliness?'

Donna became thoughtful as she considered the

question. It had no special significance, she realised. He was merely asking from casual curiosity. And then she recalled what Beryl had said about Carmen's intense desire for the large and imposing house in Taupo. It was enough to help her find a reply.

'Well?' he prompted. 'You don't seem to be able to come up with an answer. I presume your silence means that you also would be bored and lonely. Don't be afraid to admit it.'

'I've no intention of doing so. You see, Carmen and I probably have different characters.'

'You can say that again.'

'I mean, Carmen prefers to *have* things, while I prefer to *do* things.'

He looked at her uncertainly. 'Tell me more.'

'From the little I've heard I suspect that Carmen's *possessions* rule her, whereas I'd rather try to *achieve* something.'

He gave a light laugh. At the same time, his hand left the back of the settee to fondle her ear and brush her cheek with the tips of his fingers.

His touch sent her pulses racing but she remained calm as she said, 'Why do you laugh? Am I wrong about Carmen?'

'Oh no, you're dead right. It's the thought of her doing things round this quiet place that amuses me. I'd also be interested to hear what you could hope to achieve?'

'Aubrey achieved something,' she pointed out.

'Ah yes, but for him the place had potential. We're discussing what *you* could do.'

His fingers were now stroking her neck but she ignored them as she said with a hint of defiance, 'I'd begin by learning how to run this place efficiently. You won't have Beryl for ever, you know. The time will come when someone will have to take over from her.'

He frowned. 'I'm well aware of that horrible fact but I push it away every time it raises its wretched head. How I'd have managed without Beryl three years ago I hate to think.' Then, in an altered tone, 'It would content you to run Aubrey's Place?'

'No. I'd also learn a craft, like painting or spinning raw wool from the fleece. Something creative for relaxation——' She paused thoughtfully, then asked, 'Couldn't Carmen have done something similar to keep herself occupied——?'

Her words faded as she became aware that his fingers had unfastened the top button of her gown, then she waited in breathless silence as she felt his fingers slide towards the second button. She knew he was watching her intently, and she felt sure he intended to kiss her. Anticipation almost caused her to tremble as her mind jumped ahead, certain that he would unfasten the third and fourth buttons, and that his hand was about to find its way beneath her gown to hold and fondle her breast. Already her nipples were tautly erect, waiting for the gentle touch of his fingers, which suddenly paused as he gave an unexpected chuckle.

'You wonder why Carmen couldn't do any of those things? The answer is simple. She's too lazy to learn.'

Donna was conscious of intense anticlimax. He could unfasten her buttons, yet all the time his mind had been centred upon Carmen. It was like being lifted up to the heights—then dropped with a thud.

# CHAPTER SIX

DONNA took a deep breath to clear the confusion from her mind, then, keeping her voice steady, she queried, 'Are you saying that Carmen had no intention of learning to run this place?'

'None whatever. Despite any staff at her disposal, it would have meant attending to other people, and Carmen's mind doesn't work that way. She expects other people to attend to her.'

'But when you married her, weren't you aware that she'd become bored and lonely?'

'I must have had smoke in my eyes,' Grant admitted gloomily, and suddenly his hand jerked away from the region of her dressing-gown buttons. It was as though he had changed his mind about unbuttoning any more.

The action caused her to give a forced laugh while her fingers refastened the buttons. 'No doubt it'll gather to cloud your vision again. The moment she arrives it'll billow out in front of you. You'll become completely blind——'

'Aren't you getting the whole picture out of focus? Have you forgotten I've asked for your help while she's here?'

Her eyes were wide as she turned to regard him seriously. 'No, I haven't forgotten. But I also suspect that any help I give you will merely allow you to play for time while you make up your mind. You haven't seen Carmen for three years. She may have changed.'

He shook his head. 'I'm afraid not. The basic characters of people don't change. They may appear to be different, but beneath the façade they're exactly the same.'

'Well, you obviously know and understand Carmen's faults, yet you're anxious to see her again. Doesn't that speak for itself?'

'You're way off base,' he rasped.

'I doubt it. But at the same time you don't intend to be rushed into taking up the old relationship,' she pursued, 'and that's where I come in. You'll be using me to keep her at bay.' The certainty of it made her angry, causing her voice to rise slightly. 'Honestly, I feel so exasperated with myself. I don't know why I agreed—I don't know why I'm being such a fool——'

She stopped, furious with herself for betraying her inner frustration because this would let him know she'd been disappointed. Now he would guess she'd been waiting for him to kiss her, he'd *know* she'd been waiting for him to progress further than the buttons. Not that she would have allowed him to go *far*, of course. Oh no, definitely not!

'You're tired,' he said softly, his grey eyes narrowing as they regarded her intently. 'You should go to bed.'

'How right you are,' she responded crisply, making an effort to control her irritation and feeling as though she'd been dismissed. A swift movement brought her to her feet and, picking up the tray with its empty coffee mugs and sandwich plate, she went towards the kitchen with all the dignity she could muster.

But later, as she lay in her bed, sleep eluded her for a long time. Grant's face hovered clearly in the darkness above her head and, despite the shortness of their acquaintance, she knew she liked him more than any man she'd ever met. You only *like* him, you poor idiotic fool, she warned herself. It's just that he's so handsome, and that there's something about him which really appeals to you—and you've never met anyone quite like him before. But don't worry—as soon as you leave this place you'll forget all about him.

At the same time, she knew that Grant Armitage was

not a man to be easily forgotten and, although she whispered the words aloud, they failed to reassure her. She knew without a shadow of doubt that she would never forget Grant, and that she was about to be faced by the problem of getting him out of her mind before he got into her heart. Or had he found his way there already? *Of course not*——

She also knew she enjoyed the environment and atmosphere of Aubrey's Place. The lakeside fishing lodge held a charm of its own, and it needed little stretch of imagination to believe that Aubrey's spirit rested among the massed reds and golds of the trees he had planted so long ago. The memory of him was alive because Grant and Roy kept it that way, and already Donna was beginning to feel as if she herself had known the old man.

She slept at last, falling into a troubled slumber where dreams took her out into a storm that forced her to push against wind and rain. It was a relief to awaken, although she was gripped by the fanciful notion that perhaps she was about to be faced by her own personal storm. Imagination working overtime, she told herself, buttoning her dressing-gown before going to see Jodie.

A quick survey showed that Grant had already left for the office, again before she was even awake, and when she reached Jodie's door she could only stand and gaze at the child. Doc Fraser's prophecy had been correct. Jodie was indeed a sight to behold.

More spots had come out on her face, which had taken on a slightly bloated and swollen appearance, while further examination revealed the rash becoming well established on her limbs and body. Nevertheless Jodie seemed to be brighter in herself because she was now sitting up in bed surrounded by her new books.

'Daddy gave them to me before he left for the office,' she told Donna. 'He said I was to be very quiet because you were still asleep.'

Donna smiled. 'He must have been guessing. He

wouldn't know I was still asleep.'

'Yes, he did. He went in and looked at you,' Jodie argued. 'I *know* he went in your room.'

Donna was startled. 'How do you know?'

'Because your door creaks. It makes a funny little noise when somebody opens it. Daddy says it's a mouse door.'

Donna felt stunned. Surely Grant hadn't been to her room to stare at her while she slept? She smiled and said, 'You're probably imagining things, dear.'

'*I am not.*' Jodie glared at her angrily. 'I heard the door. Daddy *did* go into your room.'

'We'll have to find some oil for the hinges,' Donna told her, determined not to be perturbed. Obviously, Grant had looked in to say he was leaving for the office.

She then showered and dressed in a pair of dark brown trousers and matching jerkin that went over an apricot wool jersey. Jodie was persuaded to have a breakfast of cereal and milk, and then Donna tidied the apartment. It was as she finished making Grant's bed that she felt the prickling sensation of being watched and, straightening her back, she turned round to face a woman who stood staring at her from the doorway. There was no need to ask who she was because the likeness to herself was unmistakable. Carmen had arrived!

They stood glaring at each other in an attitude of appraisal, during which Donna noticed that Carmen's make-up was fairly heavy, especially about the eyes where tiny lines were beginning to show. Also, while waiting for her to speak. Donna had time to observe the chic black and white suit that gave its wearer an air of fashion-conscious sophistication. The high-heeled Italian-made shoes and matching handbag must have cost the earth, she thought, while the expensive white wide-brimmed hat looked suitable for the Royal enclosure at Ascot.

Carmen was the first to speak. 'Who are you?' she demanded, coming further into the room.

'I'm Donna—Donna Dalrymple.'

The hazel eyes narrowed slightly as they took in Donna's appearance. '*Dalrymple*? Is it possible we're related?' Then, brushing the thought aside, 'I suppose Beryl's given you a job here.'

'In a way, that's correct,' Donna agreed.

Carmen looked about the room. 'Everything looks the same,' she remarked with satisfaction. 'Are you supposed to have dusted that dressing-table?' She took elegant model-like steps towards the piece of furniture which was scattered with personal items belonging to Grant.

Donna gave a small shrug as she met Carmen's eyes in the mirror. 'I'll probably get around to doing it in time.'

'You appear to be very sure of your job,' the other remarked sharply, her delicate brows rising.

Donna refused to be ruffled. 'I have all day in which to do it. My time is my own, you understand.'

Carmen's eyes widened as they continued to stare at her in the mirror. 'No, I do not understand. You can't possibly stay up here all day.'

'Why not?' Donna was secretly amused.

'Because—well, naturally you must have work to do downstairs unless——' She fell silent as a thought appeared to strike her, causing her to ask abruptly, 'What are you to Grant?'

'What is any woman to any man?' Donna returned enigmatically, then she smiled in a friendly manner. 'I presume you're Carmen?'

'Of course I'm Carmen. You probably know that Grant is expecting me. Didn't he tell you to prepare the spare room?'

'Not exactly——'

'But he knows I intend to come home.'

'I don't think he understands that at all. Didn't your letter say you were coming to see Jodie?'

'I am not just coming to *see* her,' Carmen corrected

sharply. 'I'm coming to take care of her. This is her home, so naturally I'll stay here with her.'

'You mean you've come back to live with Grant?'

'I've come *home* to live with Grant. There's a subtle difference which should be clear to anyone—even to someone with limited intelligence.'

'Are you suggesting I'm someone with limited intelligence?'

Carmen lifted delicate shoulders. 'That depends.'

'Upon what?' Donna regarded her steadily.

'Upon your aspirations towards Grant, of course. I trust you haven't any—er—leanings in that direction?'

'I can't see that it would be any business of yours—Mrs Sloane,' Donna said pointedly.

'My days as Mrs Sloane are numbered,' Carmen declared, her mouth hardening.

'You have another divorce in view?' Donna asked.

'If it suits me.' Carmen swung away from the mirror to face Donna squarely. 'Not that *that's* any business of *yours*. Well, now that we understand each other I'll go down and ask Roy to carry my bags up the stairs. I'll tell Beryl I'll not be needing the end motel and that I'll move into Grant's guest room. Just to begin with, of course.' She sent Donna a broad smile. 'You might see that it's in order for me.'

Donna kept her temper under control. 'I'm afraid the guest room is already occupied. I'm sleeping in it,' she told Carmen blandly.

Carmen glared at her angrily. '*You* are sleeping up here? *Why*—may I ask?'

'You'll have to wait and learn that for yourself,' an imp prompted Donna to say evasively.

'Are you married to him? No, of course not—otherwise you wouldn't be in the guest room. Besides, I'd have heard if Grant had remarried.'

Donna shook her head.

'And you're not engaged to him—at least, you're not

wearing a ring of any description.'

'We're not engaged,' Donna admitted, 'although one never knows,' she added, remembering she had promised to play a part.

'You'd be wiser to forget any such ideas,' Carmen snapped. 'In the meantime you can move yourself out of that guest room. I'll settle into it and take care of my own dear little girl. What time does the school bus get here? She hadn't started school when I left.'

'You mean when you *deserted* her? In any case there's no need to wait for the school bus. You can start right now.'

Carmen was startled. 'What do you mean?'

'She's not at school. She's here, in the apartment.'

'She is? Then why——?'

'Why hasn't she come running to see who has arrived? Two reasons, probably. The first is that she's not well and has been given strict instructions to stay in bed. Secondly, she has a pile of new books and is no doubt engrossed in them. She can enjoy books for her age group, you know. She's six now.'

Carmen gave a gasp of disbelief. 'My baby—*six*—I can hardly believe it. Where is she?'

'In her bedroom, of course.'

'Her bedroom—why didn't you tell me at once? You're deliberately keeping me from her.' Carmen's voice became accusing as she hurried into the passage, her high heels causing her to take tiny steps.

Donna followed, reaching the passage as Carmen came to an abrupt halt at Jodie's door, and in time to see her reaction.

'My oath—*what's the matter with her*?' It was almost a shriek as Carmen recoiled visibly and backed away towards the living-room. 'She's one great mass of ghastly spots——'

'Yes, that's what happens with measles.'

'*Measles!* They're *catching*—you should have warned

me the moment I got here.' She was obviously shaken.

'They're not so dangerous if you've already had them. I'm sure Jodie will be delighted to know you're here to take care of her.'

'*But I haven't had them*, and if you imagine I'm going into that room you're off your head. I can't go near her. *I might catch them.*'

Donna's anger rose. 'Shall I tell you something? That poor child has been longing for her own mother to come to her.'

'In that case, she can hurry up and get well. I'll take care of her then, and not one moment before the spots have gone.' Carmen's voice had taken on a note of hard determination.

'Don't you love your own little daughter?'

'Of course I do. I've come home to her, haven't I?'

Donna looked at her doubtfully. 'Are you sure you haven't had measles? You could have forgotten if you had them when very young.'

'I'm positive—but quite apart from that fact, sickness always gives me the horrors. I can't cope with it. I'm afraid I could never have taken up nursing.' Her nose wrinkled with delicate distaste. 'You see, it's the *smells* of hospitals—and I'm so—so very *fastidious.*'

'So in the meantime you're happy for me to remain in the guestroom?' Donna found difficulty in hiding her amusement.

Carmen's eyes swept over Donna while she considered the question. 'Are you a trained nurse?' she asked at last.

'No, although I've completed first aid courses and I work in a doctor's surgery.'

'Pooh, that's nothing. In my opinion, Jodie needs professional care and I shall see that she gets it. I shall insist upon Grant finding a nurse—someone much more mature than yourself—and then you can go back to your kitchen-maid job——' She stopped abruptly to send

Donna a sharp glance. 'What was that you said about working in a doctor's surgery? I thought you said you work here.'

'Correction. You presumed I work here. As it happens, I'm merely helping out while Jodie is ill.' She explained about her interrupted holiday.

Carmen showed little interest or sympathy. 'Really? Too bad,' was all she said as she went towards the back door. 'But don't fret, you'll be able to continue as soon as we've found a nurse to replace you.' She began to descend the steps.

Donna spoke from above her. 'Grant has already made unsuccessful efforts to find a nurse,' she felt compelled to say.

Carmen looked back at her. 'Then he couldn't have searched very far. I'll make sure he finds someone—just you wait and see.'

Donna watched her disappear round the corner of the building. What would be Grant's reaction to her presence? she wondered. Would his planned phoney advances towards herself be put into action, or would they be forgotten and swept aside by a rekindling of his old love for Carmen? It was strange that she should feel so depressed about it.

Jodie's voice called to her as she came in and closed the door. 'Donna, a lady came and looked at me. Who was she?'

'Oh, she's someone who—who came to talk to Daddy. You'll see her again when you're better.'

Jodie's eyes became round. 'Did she run away?'

Donna sighed. 'Nearly, but not quite. We wouldn't like her to catch your measles, would we?' She couldn't bring herself to tell Jodie her own mother had just refused to take care of her. It made her feel sad, although she was thankful that Carmen did not return to Grant's apartment that day.

The only other person she saw was Roy, who came up

the inside stairs with a load of food to carry them over the long weekend. 'The place has filled up for Easter,' he told her as he dumped fresh vegetables on the kitchen bench. 'It's only Thursday, but already there are long rubber waders hanging from the hooks outside every door of the lodge.'

Donna sent him an enquiring glance. '*Every* door?'

'Well, every unit except the one occupied by Super-bitch. I believe she came up to see the young one.'

'Yes, she did take a peep at Jodie,' Donna admitted.

'But not much more, I'll be bound.' A hint of anger crossed Roy's usually cheerful face. 'When she came downstairs she tore strips off Beryl because she hadn't hired a trained nurse from the beginning. But Beryl stood up to her. She told Madam to get down the road herself to see if she could find one. We're mighty thankful to have had you here, and Beryl told her so in no uncertain terms!

When Roy's short, sturdy figure had disappeared down the stairs Donna filled in the rest of the day by attending to Jodie and by observing the activities round the lodge. She was not even remotely bored, as so much seemed to be going on, and she was intrigued by the ease with which cabin cruisers were launched into the lake by cars backing their craft-bearing trailers down ramps towards the water until the vessel could be floated off.

From the balcony she heard the revving of motors as various-sized launches made their way out towards the deeper waters of the lake, and suddenly it dawned upon her that Grant also possessed a launch. It meant that tomorrow he would be away on it from an early hour, and again she would see little of him. Well, so what?

So he was due for his Easter break, she reminded herself. The small laundry next to the back door contained his long rubber waders, and a miscellany of gear. Fishing on the lake was something he'd been looking forward to, so how could she expect him to spend the time by sitting in the apartment—especially with the sound of all those launches floating up from the lake?

No doubt he'd take Carmen with him. The thought depressed her, and once it had taken root in her mind she found difficulty in disregarding it. And no matter how she tried to occupy herself, the vision of Grant out on the lake with Carmen rose to taunt her. How much fishing would they do? she wondered with a sense of irritation.

Eventually, after a restless evening of watching television in which she had no interest, she made sandwiches in readiness for his late return. And as she didn't intend to be caught waiting for him at the window, she drew the heavy curtains but left a narrow gap. Then, with only the standard lamp casting a dim light over the large room, she was able to observe the passing cars without being seen.

It was almost ten-thirty before she saw lights turn into the lodge driveway and, hastening to peep from the kitchen window, she was rewarded by the sight of red tail-lights glowing in his garage.

She also noticed that, for the convenience of guests, the large yard was illuminated by electric bulbs attached to the back of the building, and by their light Donna saw the figure of a woman run towards Grant as he emerged from his garage. Of course, it was Carmen. No doubt she'd been waiting for him, watching for his car to turn into the drive just as she herself had been doing.

Donna watched as Carmen flung herself against Grant, clinging to him frantically and raising her face for his kiss. He brushed her cheek with his lips, then gently removed her arms from about his body. They stood talking for a short time, then she took his arm as though to draw him towards her unit at the end of the lodge, and, from her vantage point at the kitchen window, Donna sensed very little reluctance on Grant's part as he went with his ex-wife.

Frustrated, she ate some of the sandwiches, then put the rest in the fridge, almost slamming the door. A quick peep told her that Jodie was well covered and sleeping soundly, and then she went to bed where she lay feeling very wide awake—and very irritable. Deep disappointment was her real trouble, but this she refused to admit, even to herself. Nor did she have any idea of what time he came in, except that she suspected he was with Carmen for *ages*.

Next morning she was careful to greet him with a cheerful smile. 'You were very late in coming home last night,' she remarked in a casual manner.

'Yes, I was waylaid.'

'So I noticed—from the kitchen window.' *Fool*, she said to herself. Why did you have to tell him that?

He grinned. 'You saw me come home?'

'I did.' It was difficult to disguise her peevishness.

'You continued to wait up for me?'

'Of course not. I went to bed,' she snapped.

'Wise girl.' Then, without making excuses for his lengthy visit to the end motel room he asked. 'Have we thinly sliced bread for sandwiches?'

'Yes. Roy brought it. Would you like me to make some for you?'

'Thank you. Tomato for preference. Enough for two people; and you could also hard-boil some eggs.

'Two people?' Her brows rose as she glanced at him.

'Yes. I'm taking Carmen out on the lake.'

Her heart felt heavy as she said, 'Roy also brought a cooked chicken. Perhaps you'd like to take that as well.' It was difficult to keep the scathing note from her voice. *Carmen*. It was just as she'd guessed—he was taking *Carmen*.

'That'll be excellent,' he grinned. 'We'll enjoy chicken.'

'Wouldn't Carmen prefer to cook the fish you catch?' she asked. 'I presume there are cooking facilities on board——'

'Naturally, there's a good primus stove, but any fish I

catch will be brought home.'

'For me to cook, I suppose,' she snapped, feeling cross.

'That's right—thank you for offering.'

She watched as he ran down the back stairs, the sun shining on his thick, dark hair. There was a suppressed excitement about him, reminding her of a small boy who had been let out of school. Was this because Carmen had returned, or because he was suddenly free to go out on the lake?

She continued to watch as his car was backed out of the garage, turned and then reversed towards its neighbouring shed. Roy appeared and began to open large double doors, and a few minutes later a trailer bearing a large launch was attached to the car's tow-bar. As it was drawn from the shed she read the name on the bow. *Aquarius*.

Grant smiled up at her, his attitude brimming with pride. 'There she is—all shipshape and ready to go. Isn't she neat?'

Donna was still feeling cross. 'Very smart—except for her name.'

He looked nonplussed. 'What's wrong with her name? It's a sign of the zodiac.'

'I'm aware of that. Aquarius is represented by a man pouring water. I hope it doesn't mean you'll have to bail out.'

'That'll be the day,' he flung at her.

Irritated, she returned to the kitchen where she took the chicken from the fridge, put eggs to be hard-boiled into a pot and began to make tomato sandwiches.

Carmen arrived a short time later looking smartly nautical in slim, white pants, a navy and white sailor top and peaked cap. It was easy to see she had come prepared to go out on the lake with Grant. Peering into the hamper, she said, 'What shall we drink?'

'Tea or coffee, I suppose,' Donna replied. 'Grant said there's a primus on board.'

Carmen laughed. 'As if I didn't know that detail! I'm talking about something more interesting than tea or coffee.' She made her way to the living-room cocktail cabinet, then returned with a bottle of wine which she added to the hamper. 'It's to celebrate,' she explained, casting a superior smile towards Donna.

'Oh? What would you be celebrating?'

'My return, of course. As I've already told you, I've come home.'

'But—aren't you married to—to somebody else?'

'That'll be all over after I've been sleeping with Grant for a while,' she informed Donna blatantly. 'Then, as soon as my divorce goes through, we'll be married again. I'll settle down to family life with my little. girl—and Grant.'

Donna was lost for words. Family life was what she'd been preaching. The sacredness of the family unit was something she'd held up as being ideal, but Beryl's words concerning her own family made this seem an impossible state to attain—especially with Carmen being a member of it. And suddenly all her previous desires for family vanished. Even the word sounded hollow.

As though to prove this point Jodie appeared at the kitchen door. 'Is Daddy going out in the boat?'

Carmen gave a shriek of alarm. 'Go back to bed at once—don't you dare come near me—you're all spotty——'

Grant, who had just come up the stairs, spoke ironically. 'Carmen, as a loving mother you sure take the bun.'

'Do you want me to catch measles?' she hissed at him.

'You'd be interesting to watch,' he returned casually.

Jodie advanced into the kitchen, her eyes round as they stared at Carmen. 'Did Daddy say you are my Mummy? Has Santa Claus been?' Her voice rose in a wail. 'I didn't see him—*I wanted to see him.*'

Carmen backed away from her. *'Don't come near me*——'

Jodie stared at her wordlessly, her eyes filling with tears before she turned and ran back to her bedroom.

Donna's heart went out to the child. Was Carmen really her mother? How could she be so heartless?

Grant said coldly, 'You were here yesterday. Doesn't the child know who you are?'

Carmen shrugged. 'Not unless Donna told her. Surely you wouldn't expect me to take risks by pawing over someone with *measles*?'

'Knowing you, I suppose not.' He went to the bench to inspect the contents of the hamper. 'Everything we need appears to be here—even to a bottle of wine.' He turned to Donna. 'Thank you for being so thoughtful—my dearest.'

The endearment shook her. 'Oh, Carmen put that in. Apparently you're celebrating her return.'

'Are we indeed? I didn't know.' He then took Donna in his arms and kissed her lovingly. 'It's another day away from you, my darling, but this won't last for ever.'

Her arms clung to him with a desperation she was unable to control. 'I'll be waiting for you to come home,' she said, knowing she meant every word.

He held her even closer and kissed her again, his lips lingering upon her own as though unwilling to leave them. 'Darling, start watching for me late in the afternoon. That will have given me time to run Carmen round the lake and to do a few hours of fishing.'

'Take care—darling,' Donna pleaded, looking up into his face. 'I'll be watching—and waiting for you,' she said again.

'You will?' He stared into her face intently, almost as though searching for the truth of her words.

She nodded, unable to speak.

'Then I'll be sure to take care.' Once more his lips found hers, then he released her abruptly and picked up the hamper. 'OK, Carmen, let's get this trip over.'

But Carmen looked as though she'd been turned into a pillar of salt. Obviously shaken by this unexpected display of affection, her jaw had sagged noticeably, while her face had become drained of its colour. Only her eyes were alive, and they glittered angrily as she left the kitchen to follow Grant down the stairs.

Donna went through to the front balcony where she stood and watched *Aquarius* being launched into the lake with Roy's assistance. She could still feel Grant's arms about her and, while his embrace had surprised her, she realised she should have expected it because it was part of the protective wall he'd been building between Carmen and himself. This was what the sessions of practice had been all about, a fact she'd be wise to remember.

As for the wall—how long would it stand? Would it have collapsed by the time they reached home this evening? she wondered as she watched Carmen climb into the launch before it went near the water. The trailer was then backed down the concrete ramp towards the lake until *Aquarius* floated sufficiently to leave its cradle.

And then the sight of Grant scrambling over the bow caused her breath to quicken, filling her with an impulsive desire to rush down to the water's edge and plead with him to *guard the wall*. But if she did so he'd think she'd gone completely dotty, therefore she remained on the balcony, watching while Roy held the line that prevented the craft from floating out of reach before Grant was aboard. And then churning water at the stern told her the motor was throbbing.

Donna watched *Aquarius* grow smaller as the launch made its way out on to the lake. She was beset by emotions she found difficult to understand and, while she admitted to being gripped by a bitter jealousy, she was unable to find a reason for her intense misery. The tears that sprang to her eyes and rolled down her cheeks were dashed away angrily and, while she tried to ignore the depth of yearning raging within herself, she faced a question she was afraid to answer.

Surely, in this short time, she hadn't fallen in love with Grant Armitage?

She shied away from the thought like a startled foal. No, of course not—she wouldn't even consider it. When did she meet him? *Last Monday?* That was only five days ago. She couldn't possibly fall in love with a man in so short a time. She was being completely ridiculous, and the sooner she came to her senses the better.

But as the day advanced the conviction grew stronger, until at last she began to admit to herself that yes—she was *very fond* of him. If he brought fish home she'd be pleased to cook it for him. She'd even do her best to be pleasant to Carmen. But as for being in love with him— she would certainly not admit to it. At least—not yet. The whole question had to be kept in perspective.

In the meantime, all she had to do was keep her head until Jodie was well enough to be taken care of by her mother, and this would now be only a matter of days. And then she herself would disappear, Donna decided. She would carry her bags downstairs, say goodbye to Beryl and Roy, then get into her car and be on her way.

Her departure would force Grant to become closer to Carmen. Perhaps he'd sink back into his earlier relationship with her, discovering that his old love for her was still alive and simmering within the depths of his heart. The wall he was so determined to erect between them would automatically crumble.

It was afternoon when Jodie began to question Donna. The child had become engrossed in one of her new books which consisted of illustrated clothing to be cut out and placed on a cardboard doll. Tags had to be turned back to hold the glamour garments in place, and as Jodie's small fingers worked she looked up to ask, 'Did you see Santa Claus?'

Donna paused in the act of picking up scraps of paper. 'Well, I didn't actually see a tubby fellow wearing a red suit.'

Jodie sighed. 'Nobody ever sees him. Did he bring that lady?'

'It's possible,' Donna prevaricated.

'Daddy said she's a loving mother that takes buns. Where does she take them?'

'I—I don't know.' Donna found difficulty in hiding a smile.

'I like that lady,' Jodie said wistfully, 'but she keeps telling me to go away from her.'

'It's only while you've got spots,' Donna assured her. 'When they've gone I'm sure she'll love you very much.'

'*Goody, goody*——' Jodie's eyes glowed in happy anticipation.

# CHAPTER SEVEN

DONNA stood on the front balcony, her anxiety growing as her eyes scanned the lake for a sign of *Aquarius*. She glanced at her watch for the hundredth time. *Nearly six o'clock*. Above her the sky was clear, the wide belt of salmon-pink bordering the horizon promising a frosty night. The water was fairly calm, therefore she did not fear actual danger for *Aquarius* and the two people on board—it was the fact that Grant might not *want* to come home. It was possible he might be more than happy to remain out there with Carmen.

Donna's newly awakened emotions were prodded by forked jealousy and, as she strained her eyes against the growing darkness, she was filled by a sudden relief as a distant spot on the water heralded the approach of the vessel. Then, not wishing to be caught watching for them, she left the balcony and hurried to the kitchen where she hastily attended to vegetables for the evening meal.

Trout—they were sure to bring in trout, for which the lake was famous, and she raked her mind searching for ways in which to deal with it. Of course, she could cut it up and fry it in a pan, but that would be too mundane. Carmen would be derisive. *Can't you do any better than that?* she'd demand scathingly.

But when Grant came up the back stairs he was alone. He appeared to be tired and frustrated, and he carried one lone trout. 'That's all we caught,' he informed her gloomily.

'At least you hooked one,' she sympathised. 'It looks quite large.'

'It's only a five-pounder—and what's more, I didn't catch it. Carmen brought it in. It's her fish.'

114

'Oh, so that's what's bugging you.'

'I suppose so. She played it like an expert.'

'I thought she'd have been with you,' Donna said carefully. There'd been no greeting kiss just for practice, she noticed sadly.

'Oh, she'll arrive for a meal——'

'But not in time to cook the trout,' Donna flashed at him.

'You can be sure of that. She's gone to her motel for a shower and change of clothes. In the meantime I'll go downstairs to scrape and gut this fellow.'

By the time he returned with the cleaned trout Donna had recalled her mother's method of baking a whole fish. A quick search soon revealed a roll of aluminium foil, which was laid in a large flat baking dish. It was spread with layers of brown sugar, finely chopped onion, slices of bacon, pepper and salt and a sprinkling of Worcester sauce.

Grant watched with interest as she placed the trout on one half of the foil, then folded the other half across the top and tucked in the edges. 'Where did you learn that mixture?' he asked.

'My mother does it this way,' she told him casually. Bless you, Mother, she added silently to herself.

Grant made no further comment. He went to the bathroom to shower, and when he reappeared his leisure wear was smart, while his aftershave held an aroma of pinewoods.

Carmen arrived as he was pouring pre-dinner drinks. Her emerald-green dress of clinging wool jersey hugged her hips, the provocatively low-cut bodice emphasising the fullness of her breasts. It made Donna feel that her own simple jersey and skirt lacked interest, but she had no intention of changing to compete with Carmen.

The latter beamed at Grant as she took the glass he offered on a small silver tray. 'Scotch on the rocks—how well you remember every little thing about me.' She tinkled the ice in her glass. 'Thank you, darling, for a wonderful day.' Then, sniffing the air delicately, she stared at Donna. 'Do I smell my trout cooking?'

Donna sipped her sherry. 'You do. It's in the oven being baked.'

Carmen sent her a superior smile. 'I wondered if you'd know what to do with it. You've stuffed it, of course?'

Donna regarded her steadily. 'No, I haven't stuffed it,' she replied in calm tones.

Carmen put her glass down on the coffee table, then turned upon Donna angrily. 'Are you saying you're *ruining* my beautiful trout—that you haven't stuffed it with breadcrumbs and butter and onion and mixed herbs and nutmeg and—and lemon juice and egg——?' She seemed to run out of words as she paused gasping for breath.

'You've forgotten the parsley, pepper and salt,' Donna laughed, determined she would not allow Carmen to rile her.

But Carmen was not amused as she swung round to face Grant. 'Really, my dear—it's too bad. I was so anxious for you to enjoy a lovely trout meal after our marvellous day out on the lake, but now heaven alone knows what you'll be eating!'

'Something tells me you might be surprised,' he assured her drily.

'*Really?*' Carmen's eyes flashed green as she turned them upon Donna. 'What exactly have you done with it?'

'I've done trout Montana,' Donna told her casually. 'Some of the people in Montana do it this way when they go camping—except that they use bear fat. My mother has a friend who sent her the recipe.'

'Then it had better be good,' Carmen snapped.

It was. Donna knew moments of anxiety as she lifted the fish from the oven, but when the tin foil was turned back the fish surpassed even her own expectations.

Grant leaned across the table and patted her hand. 'I compliment you, my dear. I've never tasted a better trout.'

Carmen said nothing, her answer being to leave most of it untouched on her plate.

However, the subject of the fish came to an abrupt halt when Jodie appeared in the living-room. She came in quietly to stand beside Carmen's chair, strands of her red hair falling across round hazel eyes that stared from a face covered with crimson spots. 'Did Santa Claus bring you here?' she asked.

Carmen drew back from her, then appealed to Grant. 'What on earth is she talking about?'

'For Pete's sake, the child hasn't got the plague,' Grant snapped. 'It's only measles.'

'Which I have no intention of catching,' Carmen reminded him. 'Nor do I want to be near them—so please stand well away from me, Jodie. Now then, what's this business about Santa Claus?'

Grant left the table and went to his desk. When he returned he handed Carmen the letter Jodie had written to Santa Claus. 'Perhaps this will help you to work it out for yourself,' he drawled.

Carmen read the few lines in silence, then turned to Jodie. Her tone softened as she asked, 'You really want your mother to come home? You've been missing her?'

Jodie nodded, then gazed at Carmen intently. 'Are you my mother?'

But Carmen's eyes were still glued to the letter. 'In his heart Daddy wants her to come home,' she read, her voice vibrating with triumph. 'Daddy told you to say that?'

Jodie shook her head. 'No, Donna said to put that. She told me how to spell heart——'

Donna stared at the table, wishing she could scrub that line.

'Don't read too much into it,' Grant warned. 'Donna was merely helping the child.'

Carmen sent him a roguish glance. 'Why not admit she hit upon the truth?'

Jodie began to hop with impatience. 'Are you my

mother?' she asked again.

There was a long moment of silence before Carmen
said, 'Yes, I'm your mother.'

'Goody, goody,' Jodie shouted huskily. 'Can I call my
new doll Carmen? I want her to have the same name as
you——'

Her mother was delighted. 'Of course. You must show
her to me, but not before you are better.'

Grant was puzzled. 'What new doll is this, Jodie?'

'She's the one with dresses cut out of the book. She's
only a paper doll——'

'Ah, how very appropriate,' Grant murmured.

Donna sent him a rapid glance, the barbed remark
telling her he was feeling bitter inside. Perhaps the day
out with Carmen had revived old memories, bringing
back the heartache of when she had first left him.

If Carmen noticed the remark she ignored it, her full
attention being given to Jodie. 'As you can see, I've really
come home. Now, will you please go to bed? When
you've got rid of those nasty spots we'll have lots of fun
together.'

Jodie looked at her expectantly. 'What'll we do?'

'Oh, we'll go out on the lake with Daddy, and perhaps
he'll take us both shopping in Taupo.'

Jodie's eyes shone. 'To buy presents for me?'

'Only if you're a good girl. Now off to bed at once.'

Jodie went obediently, and as she left the room
Carmen smiled at Grant. 'There now, it's all arranged,'
she said with undisguised satisfaction. 'Nobody could
possibly disappoint that child.'

'What, exactly, is arranged, Carmen?' he asked
quietly.

'Why—Jodie's situation, of course. She needs her
mother as well as her father. I'll admit I made a terrible
mistake when I went away from her, but that is about to
be rectified. I know you've always loved me, Grant—and
I know you'll forgive me. We'll take up where we left off.
It's as simple as that.'

Donna was swept by embarrassment. Carmen's statement had made her feel that she didn't even exist in the room at all, and at best, it made her aware that her presence was something they'd rather be without. She looked at Grant anxiously, wondering about his reaction to Carmen's words, and then she stood up and said, 'I'm sure you'd prefer to discuss this—this situation without my—my——'

'Without your listening ears?' Carmen supplied. 'How right you are—because naturally, this is private.'

'Sit down, Donna.' It was a quiet command from Grant. 'This also concerns you.'

'How can it possibly concern her?' Carmen's tone was indignant. 'Surely you must realise that this is between *us*.'

Grant eyed her steadily. 'You don't appear to be aware of the situation between Donna and me—or if you do suspect we have an understanding, it pleases you to ignore it.'

Carmen laughed. 'An *understanding*? What a quaintly old-world way of putting it. Are you trying to tell me that you and Donna are having an *affair*—that she's your *temporary* woman?'

Donna almost felt the blood drain from her face. 'How dare you say such a thing——' she gasped furiously.

Carmen shrugged. 'There's no need to get so uptight. Naturally, he needs a woman. Most men do.' Her lip curled as her eyes ran over Donna's face. 'And you're quite attractive, even if it pains me to say so. However, I don't believe he's in love with you.'

Grant frowned at her. 'Why should it surprise you?'

'Oh, it wouldn't *surprise* me,' Carmen returned grudgingly, 'it's just that I don't *believe* it. That display of affection when we were leaving this morning was put on for my benefit, but it didn't convince me—no, not one little bit.'

'Why not?' Grant's voice was icy.

'Because it came too suddenly,' she laughed. 'I'll admit

I was fooled for a short time, but when I began to think about it I realised it was just a hoax.'

'Is it necessary to wear our hearts on our sleeves?' Donna asked, feeling a word from her was expected.

Carmen smiled knowingly. 'No—but there is always that little something that betrays the situation between true lovers,' she pointed out shrewdly. 'There are special looks where people hold each other's gaze—there is the touch of hands—none of which I've noticed. Oh no, you can't fool me.'

'Then you've been unobservant,' Donna snapped, irritated by the other's assurance of the situation between herself and Grant.

Carmen sent her a tantalising smile. 'Have I? I don't think so. When we left the boat ramp he didn't even turn round to send you a wave. And there you were, standing on the balcony waiting for it. I almost felt sorry for you.' Her smile became even broader.

Grant sighed wearily. 'Carmen, Donna and I have been very patient with you. Last night, you pleaded for a run out in the launch and that wish was granted.'

Her eyes widened appealingly. 'Don't you understand? I had to talk to you in private. Where else could I explain the situation with Oliver?'

'You could have told me about it here.'

She sent a baleful glance towards Donna. 'With *her* listening to all my private affairs? Not likely. Besides— darling—I wanted to be alone with you.'

'Very touching,' he commented drily.

She ignored his tone as she added, 'And don't forget I need your legal advice about the best way to handle this affair. I mean, from the point of view of the law, I want it worked in the best way for—*for us.*'

Grant turned to Donna, his manner apologetic. 'My dearest, I'm sorry you've had to listen to this—that you're being subjected to this sort of unpleasantness. I can only suggest that Carmen is overtired. She isn't thinking straight. She's had the hassle of travel across the Tasman, and she's worn out both mentally and physically——'

'Don't you dare say I'm not thinking straight!' Carmen broke in angrily. 'Nor am I worn out, as you suggest——'

Grant ignored the interruption as he explained to Donna, 'She's lied to her husband by saying she's taking a break at Surfer's Paradise in Queensland, but instead of going towards sea and sun her flight brought her across that strip of water to Auckland. Then there was the long bus trip down to Taupo, followed by a day out on the lake—so you'll understand she's not quite herself.'

Donna smiled at him. 'As you say, she must be really worn out. You sit and talk to her while I make coffee.'

'Thank you, my darling.' Grant took her face between his hands. For several moments he stared down into her eyes, almost as though sending an unspoken message, and then he kissed her brow, her cheeks and her lips, brushing them gently backwards and forwards with his own as his hand stroked her jaw.

They were light caresses but they caused Donna's heart to thump. Nor did Carmen's derisive laugh have the power to take away the thrill of his touch, and, as she went to the kitchen, her pulses were still hammering.

She did not hurry with the coffee. Let them talk, she decided as she busied herself by clearing the table and stacking the plates into the dishwasher. She noticed that Grant leaned forward in serious discussion with Carmen, and although she had no wish to eavesdrop she caught the odd phrase which told her their subject concerned the Australian and New Zealand divorce laws.

She delayed taking in the coffee for as long as possible and, when she finally placed the tray with its small cups on the table, she was in time to see Carmen wipe a tear, and to hear Grant say, 'Well, that's the situation. I hope you can understand everything I've been trying to tell you.'

Carmen looked at him vaguely as she shook her head. Her attitude had changed visibly, and she now appeared to have taken on the role of the helpless little woman who

needed the arm of a strong man. 'I'm afraid most of it is
over my head,' she said at last.

Grant became impatient. 'For Pete's sake, Carmen—
you've been through most of it before.'

She looked at him hopefully. 'Perhaps I could
understand it better if you explained it to me again—
tomorrow—out on the lake.'

Donna's heart sank as she flicked a quick glance
towards Grant in an effort to gauge his reaction to this
plea. She watched him frown as he considered it, then
waited breathlessly for his reply.

Carmen took advantage of his hesitation. 'Grant,
dear—we *must* have another day together. There's so
much to be discussed—such things as where I'll live now
that I've—come *home*.' She sipped her coffee thoughtfully before bringing up another point. 'And there's
Jodie to be considered. Now that Santa Claus has
brought me back to her, she's not likely to let me go
again so easily——'

'You mean as easily as she did when she was only three
and you simply disappeared out of her life?' Grant's
voice gritted harshly.

'Please, don't keep punishing me,' Carmen
whimpered.

'Very well, but by tomorrow evening I expect a few
decisions to have been made.'

Carmen's face became wreathed in smiles. 'Oh yes, I
hope so too, Grant, dear—decisions that will affect us
both—especially as that nice judge said I could have
access to Jodie. *Remember?* That means I'll have to stay
close at hand.'

Grant looked at her without speaking.

Carmen turned to Donna, her eyes glittering with
barely concealed victory. 'Perhaps you'll be good enough
to make sandwiches for us in the morning.'

'Of course I'll do that for you,' Donna replied in a dull
voice that did nothing to disguise her depression.

'There's no need,' Grant assured her. 'We'll land at the

jetty near Taupo and I'll take Carmen to lunch at the hotel.'

'Grant, darling—how marvellous,' Carmen echoed.

'How very nice for her.' Donna's depression deepened.

Grant said, 'After lunch I'll contact Bill Adams, an estate agent.'

Carmen's brows rose. 'An estate agent?'

'To enquire about a flat you can move into.'

'But—but I thought——'

'I know exactly what you thought, Carmen. However, if you're in a flat at Taupo, Jodie will be able to live with you, or she can divide her time between us. In Taupo she'll be nearer to school, so everything will be better for her.'

He left the table, went to the phone and made a short call. As he returned to the table his decisive manner gave the impression he had the entire situation under control. A satisfied note rang in his voice as he said, 'I've made an appointment with Bill Adams. He'll see us at three o'clock.'

'Nonsense—he'll be closed for Easter,' Carmen protested.

'Holidays are his bread-and-butter days,' Grant explained. 'That's when strangers come here and are bitten with the bug of wanting to live at Taupo.' His manner became even more decisive. 'Well, now—I think it's time you returned to your motel. It's been a long day and Donna and I would like at least a few minutes of it together. So—if you don't mind——'

Carmen gave a brittle laugh. 'Actually I do mind, especially being given that silly story again. But you're right when you say I'm tired.' She sent a nervous glance towards the starlit sky that could be seen through the parted curtains. 'You'll come with me to make sure I get there safely?'

'Of course.' He stood up and accompanied her to the door.

Donna watched them go down the back stairs,

Carmen clutching his arm like a clinging vine. 'That'll be the last I'll see of him tonight,' she muttered to herself. 'Carmen will get him into her motel and there he'll stay for *hours*——'

She placed the coffee cups in the dishwasher, then turned the switch that sent the hot water gushing into it. The sound reflected the turmoil in her own mind, and as she wiped the bench she was again overcome by a raging jealousy that caused her to thump the bench in a spasm of fury. '*Stop it*—you *stupid* idiot,' she told herself aloud.

'Stop what?' Grant's voice came from behind her.

She swung round to face him. The noise of the dishwasher had enabled him to come in unheard and now she could only stare at him in a wordless stupor.

He covered the space between them and stared down into her face. 'Well? What do you intend to stop?'

She raked about in her mind for an answer, then said weakly, 'I—I must stop worrying about your situation.' The fact that it now concerned herself was something she hardly dared face.

His eyes seemed to penetrate her brain. 'You really are worrying about my situation?' he asked in a low voice.

She kept her eyes lowered as she nodded without looking at him. 'As you said, she's very determined to attain her ambitions.'

'I know that only too well. However, you have no need to worry about my problem. I have it completely under control.'

She laughed shakily. 'That's what you think. I can assure you that Carmen isn't even remotely convinced about—about us meaning anything to each other.' Why was it so difficult to utter simple words? she wondered.

He looked at her gravely. 'In that case, I suspect we need much more practice, and it had better be intense enough to enable us to *feel* closer together. Do you understand?'

She nodded in dumb agreement.

'In that way it will appear as if there really is

something between us. Love is a little like justice. It not only has to be there—it has also to be *seen* to be there. I'm afraid our brief touches have been only lukewarm.'

She looked at him apprehensively. What did he have in mind? 'It—it all sounds so clinical——'

The words died on her lips as his sudden movement swept her from her feet and up into his arms. Surprised, the unexpected action took her breath away and she could only gaze at him mutely as, almost of their own volition, her arms clung to his shoulders, then crept about his neck.

'That's better,' he murmured, his lips trailing across her face.

A rush of excitement caused her to tremble, and she closed her eyes lest he detected her inner joy shining from them. And then his lips found hers in a long and gentle kiss that was full of tenderness, although it was without passion.

Only a practice run, she reminded herself, and then, his arms tightening about her, she felt herself being carried from the kitchen. He's taking me to the settee, she thought, her mind in a whirl.

But he did not make his way towards the living-room. Instead, he carried her to his bedroom where he laid her on the wide double bed. There had been no need to switch on the light because the darkness was broken by shafts from the brilliant full moon filtering into the room, and, having deposited her on the bed, he stood back to form a shadowy silhouette against the window.

For several moments no word was spoken until, suddenly feeling foolish, she began to sit up.

'Stay there,' he commanded abruptly.

'Why?'

'I just want to look at you lying on that bed.'

'Don't you mean that you're trying to see Carmen lying on this bed? She should be easy enough to remember.' The sound of the words sent a pain through her.

'That's a stupid thing to say.' He moved to sit on the

bed beside her, and as he leaned over her he placed a hand upon her breast. 'Your heart is thumping like the proverbial sledge-hammer.'

'I'm not accustomed to being carried to bed,' she said defensively, well aware of her tingling nerves and racing pulses that sent the blood galloping through her veins.

Moonlight played on one side of his handsome face as he murmured, 'You're afraid I'm about to make love to you—to take you against your will. Be honest and admit it.'

Her face felt hot as she shook her head. 'I don't believe you're the type of man who'd rape a girl.'

'Thank you for the confidence. In that case, you won't mind if I join you.' He stood up and walked to the other side of the bed where a swift movement indicated he'd discarded his shoes. The next moment he was lying stretched beside her, although he was raised on one elbow while he continued to look down at her in silence.

The long pause enabled her to regain her composure and she could only return his gaze wordlessly until she felt compelled to say, 'Why do you watch me so intently?'

His head was slightly bent, causing his eyes to be shadowed by his brows, and when he spoke his voice was low. 'I'm implanting you in my mind. If I never see you again, this is how I shall always remember you—a moonlight madonna.'

His words filled her with quiet happiness, but she knew she must not allow them to go to her head. Nevertheless, she was unable to resist saying, 'There's a piece of music by Zdenik Fibich—a slow dreamy tune called Poem——'

'But it's more popularly known as "Moonlight Madonna". I know it. Nor shall I ever hear that haunting melody again without recalling these moments.'

She smiled at him. 'You're showing me a new side to yourself. I had no idea that at heart you're such a romantic.'

'Only during unguarded moments,' he admitted.

But at present he was on guard, she realised, because he made no move to take her in his arms, and his casual attitude enabled her to remain calm while savouring the joy of such close contact without passion. She was on his bed. *Grant's bed*—and there was something infinitely soothing about what seemed to be an intimate companionship. It was like floating on one's back in a rare patch of tepid sea water near the shore, she thought. But on those occasions the bliss was often stolen by a chilly wave that swept along to wash over one, and this happened now when, despite his recent words, she was forced to realise it was Carmen who dominated his mind.

Changing his position, Grant lay on his back and stared at the darkened ceiling while his voice came gruffly. 'I find difficulty in believing Carmen's marriage has broken up. She was so very much in love with Sloane.'

Donna had no wish to discuss Carmen, but she forced herself to ask a question. 'Did she tell you what had gone wrong between them?'

He gave a mirthless laugh. 'Did she ever? I heard nothing else all day. It was a long garbled account about Oliver and a blue-eyed blonde named Faye. There were times when Carmen contradicted herself to such an extent I could make neither head nor tail of the story, but it boils down to the fact that Oliver's eye seems to have wandered.'

'And so she has left him completely?'

'That appears to be the situation, although I might add there were times when I wondered if his faithlessness was a build-up of her own intense jealousy and vivid imagination.'

'So what do you intend to do about her?' The question slipped out despite herself.

'What do *you* think I should do?' he countered.

'You're asking *me*? Why not ask a solicitor?' she quipped.

'That smart reply is one below the belt, However, it

was an unnecessary question because I think I can follow your trend of thought without too much trouble.'

She felt nettled. 'Oh, is that so?'

'Definitely. It's easy to guess that you consider I should open my arms to her for Jodie's sake. Huh! You and your obsession with *family*. Or has that high ideal now died a natural death?'

'No, it hasn't. I still believe in the importance of family, but surely the answer to this problem lies within yourself. Either you take her back into your arms—or you send her home to Oliver.'

'I'll have to think about it,' was all he said.

The answer frustrated her, but before she could say anything further his hand lying between them on the bed found her own, clasping it in a firm hold that sent tingles up her arm and into her treacherous nerve cells.

And then he released her hand as he turned upon his side to lean above her once more, and, staring down at her his deep voice came huskily, 'Donna—the girl who longs for a family. You are indeed well named—a real madonna who can be relied upon.'

She gazed at him mutely, revelling in his admission that he found her attractive, and while there had been other men who had praised her appearance, their words had meant nothing to her. This time it was different. It was exciting.

Suddenly his arms moved to encircle her, and as he gathered her closer to his body she raised her face to meet the mouth that slowly descended upon her own. Hungry for his kiss, her lips parted, and it was in that moment that she knew she really loved him. Something deep within her snapped, allowing the knowledge to flood up into her brain, and she knew that for her there would never be anyone else.

Joyfully, she felt his fingers gently knead the muscles surrounding her shoulder-blades, then massage her back while gliding down towards her hips. Her body seemed to leap into a newly found life, quivering as spasms of desire shot through her entire being.

Her mind in a daze, she felt his hands leave her hips to move gradually upward to find their way beneath her jersey. Pushing it over her chest and sliding flimsy straps aside, his lips made their way to her bare breasts, and, while she told herself she should push him away, she was powerless to do so. Instead, she ran her fingers through his dark hair, pressing his face even closer in an ecstasy of unutterable pleasure.

Grant's lips left her breast and again found her mouth in a wild frenzy of passion that lasted until suddenly he raised his head to stare long and searchingly into her face that was still washed by moonbeams. There was no need for words between them. His masculinity and unspoken longing to make love called loudly, while her own body throbbed with yearning to respond but, even as she almost whispered a confession of her love for him, a warning voice niggled at the back of her brain—*this is not the right moment to give yourself to him*——

And indeed it was not, because at that moment the moonlit silence of the room was shattered by a cry that came from Jodie as her distressed voice called, 'Mummy—where are you, Mummy? I want to go to the loo——

The words brought a muffled expletive from Grant and a gasp from Donna as she struggled from his arms and sprang from the bed. She rushed out into the passage to be faced by a bewildered Jodie whose face was flushed, and whose eyes glistened with tears.

'Where's my mummy?' she demanded. 'I want my mummy——'

'You'll seen her in the morning,' Donna consoled gently.

'*I want her now*—I want her to take me to the loo——' Jodie's wail of anger echoed round the hall.

'I'm afraid she's asleep in her motel, so you'll have to let me take you instead,' Donna explained.

Jodie began to jump and stamp in a tantrum. '*No—no, I won't*——' she shouted defiantly. 'I don't want you to take me to the loo—I want my mummy.'

Grant came out into the passage. 'What the devil's going on?' he demanded. 'What's all this nonsense?'

'I don't want Donna,' Jodie whined. 'I want my mummy to take me to the loo——'

'Confounded rot! You're being a very naughty girl. You've been taking yourself for ages.'

'But I got measles. I gotta be took when I got measles——'

'Rubbish! Get in there at once and cut out all this racket, because I've got a phone call to make.' He frowned at his watch thoughtfully as though considering the time.

Donna glanced at her own watch. It was not far from midnight. 'Isn't it rather late to be ringing anyone?' she asked.

'Not this person.' He strode into the living-room and turned into the alcove where the phone rested on the desk.

Donna became conscious of bitter disappointment. Surely he wasn't ringing *Carmen*? But who else would be unlikely to object to a call at this hour? Carmen, she felt sure, would be delighted to receive a call from him at any hour.

She attended to Jodie and, as she tucked the child into bed once more, she remembered that the sherry glasses they'd used before dinner had been left in the living-room and were waiting to be washed. Grant was still on the phone when she went in to fetch them and, as she carried them from the room, she distinctly heard him mention Carmen's name.

So her suspicions had been correct, she decided, while waves of misery washed over her. He had felt the need to talk to Carmen—and it seemed to prove that she herself was no substitute for his ex-wife. But if his need was so urgent, why didn't he go downstairs to see her? After all, she was only as far away as the end motel.

Donna sighed, realising that no doubt he had his own

reasons for not doing so. She washed the glasses and put them away, then prepared for bed. And as she left the bathroom, the murmur of his voice came to her ears, telling her he was still on the phone, and that this was indeed a very long conversation.

Frustrated, she climbed between the sheets where her mind became filled with bitter thoughts which sent tears trickling down her face and into the pillow. *Carmen.* Had his brain been obsessed by her during the time they'd been so close to each other on the bed? In his imagination had it been Carmen, rather than herself, who had pressed his head to her breast? And had his longing for Carmen been so intense he'd been unable to resist phoning her the moment she herself had left his arms?

It was a nasty dose of medicine to swallow—but medicine was meant to cure, so perhaps the unpalatable taste of these unpleasant facts would bring her to her own senses. That was if they *were* facts, of course, but no matter how she sifted them in her mind there seemed to be no other reason for his long phone call to Carmen.

# CHAPTER EIGHT

IT WAS hours before Donna fell asleep, nor did she feel refreshed when she woke next morning. Instead her head felt heavy and, as though in sympathy with her mood, the weather had also changed overnight to present a morning of grey skies and dark clouds. A stiff breeze whipped the lake to a state of choppiness and, as she stared through the bedroom window, there were no fishing launches to be seen.

The heavy depression caused by last night's intense disappointment continued to remain with her and, as she stood under the soothing hot water of the shower, Donna told herself she was being a fool. The problem could be solved quite simply by her departure. She had only to hand over the care of Jodie to the child's mother, then get into her car and continue with her planned vacation.

Yet she knew she was unable to do this. Her newly awakened love for Grant held her to the place, tied by invisible strings that nothing on earth could break, therefore she made excuses for not leaving.

It would be like running away from a job before it was finished, she told herself. It would put an extra burden of work upon Beryl, because Carmen—being Carmen— would surely demand assistance from one she regarded as being Grant's servant. And with these reasons for remaining firmly fixed in her mind, she went to the kitchen to attend to Jodie's breakfast.

When she walked into the room she was surprised to find Grant at the bench preparing to cook bacon and scrambled eggs and, while it was difficult to keep the accusation from her voice, she managed to say calmly, 'I see you're expecting Carmen to join you for breakfast.'

He shot her a look of surprise. 'You do? What makes you so sure about it?'

'The fact that you appear to be cooking such a large amount. Besides, that long conversation you had with her must surely have ended with a *see you at breakfast touch*——' Her voice shook slightly then trailed away as jealousy gnawed at her.

'You could be mistaken, you know.'

Her heart lifted. 'I am? Carmen's not coming to breakfast?'

'No. This is for us. I thought you looked pale and tired when I saw you come out of the bathroom. I decided you need a good breakfast, so I'm preparing it.'

'Oh—thank you.' Gratitude shone from her hazel eyes.

He put sliced bread into the toaster. 'Now tell me—what makes you so sure I had a long conversation with Carmen? Were you able to hear it? I thought you'd gone to bed.'

Her chin rose slightly. 'I wasn't eavesdropping, if that's what you're suggesting, but I do know you were on the phone for ages, and I did hear you call her by name. However, it's not my business.'

'You're sure of that?' he asked quietly.

'Of course I'm sure,' she snapped.

'Yet I get the feeling it has upset you in some way.'

'Then you can get that silly idea right out of your head.' She turned away, unable to look at him lest he read the real answer in her eyes.

'Tell me the truth,' he demanded, gripping her shoulders and staring down into her face. 'Is there the remotest possibility that you could be—*jealous*?'

His suspicions horrified her, and to hear the question put into words made it even worse. She glared at him defiantly. '*Jealous*? Of you and Carmen? Huh! You've got to be out of your mind.' The last words came as little more than a squeak, for she almost choked on them.

'I see.' He released her abruptly. 'So last night didn't

mean a confounded thing to you?' His voice had become cold.

'You certainly showed it meant absolutely nothing to *you*,' she retaliated with a hiss. 'After we'd been so—so very close—you—you weren't happy until you'd phoned her and hung on her words for what seemed like *hours*.' Her eyes were now full of reproach. 'Go on—deny it if you can,' she added furiously, longing to hear him utter the words.

But the denial did not come. Instead he looked beyond her towards the door where Jodie, clutching Lulu in her arms, stood watching them. 'I smell bacon,' she said plaintively. 'I want some bacon. I want my breakfast——'

The interruption came as a welcome relief. 'You're actually *hungry*?' Donna asked with interest. 'You'll eat a good breakfast?'

Jodie nodded. 'Yes, with lots of bacon.'

'Then you'll have some. Does this mean you're beginning to feel a little better?' she pursued hopefully.

Jodie nodded, watching as a rasher was put on a plate and then cut into small pieces. 'Do I have to stay in bed?' she asked pleadingly.

'Most definitely,' Grant assured her in a stern voice.

Jodie pouted, but made no protest as Donna led her back to bed. However, she sprang out again as soon as she heard Carmen arrive, and then, facing her mother accusingly she said, 'You went away again——'

'Only for the night, dear. As soon as your nasty spots have gone I'll be here all the time—home with you and Daddy. Now go back to bed and see that you stay there.'

She's certainly very sure of herself, Donna thought bitterly. She stole a glance at Grant. A muscle in his jaw seemed to be working, but he said nothing.

Carmen moved to stand in front of him. She spun round slowly and said, 'Do you like my new suit? It's the latest style in Sydney.'

He ran critical eyes over the well cut and costly-looking garment. 'Very smart. Why are you wearing it to go out in the launch?'

'Because we're not going out in the launch,' she declared with an air of satisfaction. 'I've decided it's too rough, so we'll go out in the car instead. It's ages since I've had a closer look at those old volcanoes at the end of the lake, so I thought we'd drive south and have lunch at the Château Tongariro.'

Donna looked at Grant as she remarked, 'I could have sworn you'd made other arrangements for this afternoon.'

Carmen sent her an angry glare. 'Will you kindly shut up and mind your own business?'

'She's right,' Grant drawled. 'Have you forgotten we have an appointment at three o'clock with the estate agent in Taupo? We couldn't possibly get back in time.'

'Blast the estate agent!' Carmen snapped angrily. 'I have no intention of going near him, and if you imagine you can force me to look at flats you're very much mistaken.'

They glared at each other until, for some strange reason, Grant appeared to capitulate. Then, to Donna's intense disappointment he said, 'OK, I'll cancel the flat inspection. We'll go to Château Tongariro for lunch.'

Carmen was elated. She shot a look of veiled satisfaction towards Donna as she clasped Grant's arm and gazed up into his face. 'Thank you, darling—thank you.'

Grant removed her hands and went to the phone. They listened as he made two phone calls, one to the estate agent in Taupo and the other to reserve a table for lunch at Château Tongariro. Nor did he look at Donna as he led Carmen towards the back stairs, and in that moment she told herself she hated him. Yet at the same time she realised that this was a lie, because her love for him had settled into a deep permanency which told her she'd never be able to hate him. OK, so he longed to have his ex-wife back in his arms. There was nothing she could do about it.

As if to drive this point home, Carmen paused on the stairs to look back at Donna. 'A fine romance,' she jeered tauntingly. 'Once again, he didn't even kiss you goodbye.'

Donna could find nothing to say. She closed the back door, leaning against it while tears stung her eyes, then she went to the front balcony from where she watched the car turn south towards the three volcanoes. It was out of sight in minutes.

The iciness of the southerly wind whipped through the sleeves of her jersey while the choppy waters of the lake, the grey skies above, reflected her turbulent mind and the misery in her soul. She came in and closed the door, then went to her room where she lay on the bed and wept.

Eventually, she dragged herself from the bed and went to the bathroom where she pressed a cold wet face flannel to her red eyes and, as she stared at her reflection in the mirror above the wash-basin, she spoke to herself in a stern voice. 'You poor pathetic fool—snap out of this stupid state of depression. Find yourself something to do. *Forget that man.*'

The latter part of the advice offered to herself was not easy to follow because Grant's face hovered before her eyes most of the time. But apart from that it was easy enough to keep herself occupied, and by lunch time she had changed all the bed linen, carried the vases of wilting flowers to the kitchen, vacuumed the apartment and spent time reading to Jodie.

After listening to one story the child's face became pitiful as she asked, 'Why doesn't my mother read to me like you do?'

'Because she's afraid of catching measles,' Donna explained. 'Perhaps she hasn't had them before now.'

Jodie looked at her seriously. 'I want you to go away,'

she declared with uncompromising frankness.

Donna smiled. 'You do? Don't you like me any more?'

'No, I don't. If you go away my mother will stay with me.'

Donna laughed, refusing to take offence. 'I'm afraid you'll have to wait until your spots disappear. When they've gone I'll go too, and then you can have your mother with you all the time.'

'Goody, goody!' Jodie exclaimed, staring at her hands intently. 'When will they go?'

'Oh, they'll be with you for a few days yet—probably all next week. These things take time.'

'Do I have to stay in bed all next week?'

'No. You'll be allowed up when most of them have gone and your temperature is down to normal. Now then—I must find some fresh flowers for the living-room.'

She returned to the kitchen where the empty vases stood on the bench, then, finding a small pair of secateurs, she went down the back stairs to the flower beds where she helped herself to fresh blooms. Early frosts were beginning to take toll of the dahlias and zinnias, but the yellow and bronze chrysanthemums were still beautiful.

She carried them upstairs, and it was as she reached the landing that she heard the persistent ringing of the telephone. The flowers were hastily placed on the bench, then she hurried to snatch up the receiver. 'Hello?'

An abrupt male voice came over the line. 'Is that the residence of Grant Armitage?'

'Yes, but I'm afraid he's not here at present.'

There was a pause before the voice came again. 'Can you give him a message?'

'Yes, of course.'

'Tell him five o'clock Tuesday.'

'This is for an appointment?'

'You can call it that.'

'He won't be at the office on Tuesday. The law offices are closed all next week for a long Easter break.'

'I'm well aware of that fact. However, I reckon he'll see me. Just make sure he gets the message.'

'Very well.' It was the estate agent, she decided, and to verify this she asked, 'Would you like to leave your name so that I can tell him who called?'

But the receiver had clicked in her ear.

A rude man, she thought, to be forgiven only if he had a flat that would satisfy Carmen. No doubt the broken appointment had annoyed him, hence his abrupt manner. What was his name? Bill Adams?

She replaced her own receiver, wrote the message on the desk pad, then went back to the kitchen to arrange the flowers. By the time she'd finished she'd forgotten about the phone call apart from telling herself that no doubt Grant would guess the caller's identity and would probably get in touch with him.

The rest of the day passed without incident and, by the time Grant and Carmen arrived back at the apartment, Donna had completely regained her composure. She was also ready to face any announcement they might make— any disclosure which concerned their plans for getting together again.

However, it was early evening before they returned, and when they entered the apartment they did not appear to be full of the joy of mutual understanding. Nor did they appear to be casting secret glances at each other while surreptitiously touching hands.

In fact, the situation between them appeared to be strained and with a definite lean in the opposite direction. It became noticeable when Grant continued with the charade of taking Donna in his arms and kissing her lovingly. It was almost as if he'd forgotten that Carmen was present.

'Darling, have you missed me?' he asked in a low voice

as his lips nuzzled her ear before following the line of her jaw.

His touch sent the blood rushing to her face, causing her to tremble slightly, and as her arms went about him she was unable to stem the genuine ardour of her response as she raised her face.

'Very good—very convincing.' The whisper was barely audible, as his lips brushed hers gently, moving backward and forward in an uninhibited display of restrained passion.

The performance brought sneering laughter from Carmen who retaliated by talking to Jodie from the safe distance of the child's bedroom door. 'How would you like Mummy to come home and live with you and Daddy for ever and ever?' she asked in a voice that echoed all over the apartment.

'Goody, goody, goody!' Jodie shouted with what force she could muster, her excitement more than evident.

'Then you'll have to ask Daddy to arrange it,' Carmen advised.

Donna held her breath as she looked at Grant, waiting for him to comment upon Carmen's words.

But he only said, 'That child is on the mend. Her voice is losing its hoarseness.' He then went to the desk where the message on the pad caught his eye. 'Five o'clock Tuesday? What is this supposed to mean?'

'A man phoned,' Donna explained. 'I tried to tell him the office will be closed all next week, but he seemed to be confident that you'd see him. '

'He didn't leave his name?'

'No. I wondered if it could have been the estate agent. Perhaps something special in the way of a flat has turned up.'

'It's possible. In the meantime we'll just have to wait until five o'clock on Tuesday to see what it's all about.'

'You'll go to the office?' she asked.

'No. If it's the estate agent he knows where he can find me.'

The subject was not pursued because at that moment Carmen returned to the living-room, her eyes holding a slightly malicious glitter as they rested upon Donna. When she spoke it was with forced brightness. 'I presume you've prepared something for our evening meal? I mean—there's nothing in the oven, nor are there any savoury odours wafting from the kitchen.'

Donna sent a hasty glance towards her watch. 'No, I haven't done anything about it yet—I didn't realise it was so late.'

Carmen smiled sweetly. 'Then isn't it time you made a start?' She settled herself comfortably on the settee beside Grant as she added, 'I know we had a wonderful lunch that went on and on for ages, but now I'm sure Grant must be feeling quite peckish again.' She turned to him. 'Isn't that so, my dear?'

Grant grinned at her. 'You enjoyed your lunch?'

She leaned towards him as she said throatily, 'Darling, it was *wonderful*. Just being there with you was something out of this world. The mountains so close—the glorious views from the large windows—it's just the place for a second honeymoon.'

'The food was to your satisfaction?' he asked drily.

'*Delicious.*' A deep breath seemed to echo the memory of it.

'Jolly good. I'm glad you enjoyed it, because now it's your turn. You can prepare a meal for Donna.'

Carmen's back straightened as she sat up abruptly. 'What do you mean?' she demanded angrily.

Grant's voice became hard. 'I mean that while you were sipping wine in luxurious surroundings Donna was taking care of your sick child—a job that you yourself should have been doing. I'm sure you'll find something in the fridge or in the deep freeze.'

There was a sudden change in Carmen's expression as

her face became wreathed in smiles. '*Darling*—you're actually putting me back into my own kitchen. You wouldn't believe how many times I've thought of that dear kitchen with all its modern conveniences. Oh, yes, I'll find a meal for us. It's the first real step towards being home again.' A lithe movement took her to her feet and she left the room with quick light steps.

Donna began to giggle. 'You can't win,' she murmured. 'She gets her own way every time.' And although the thought caused a surge of misery, she was unable to resist adding, 'I wonder how long it will be before that second honeymoon takes place.'

His voice became cold. 'Are you implying that in reality I want it to take place?'

'To be honest, I can't help wondering about it. The signs certainly point that way.'

'*Signs?* What signs? What are you talking about?'

'Was it necessary for you to spend the whole long day with her?' Aching jealousy wrenched the question from her.

'Yes. I had two good reasons for spending the day with her.'

'Oh? One of them being that you just wanted to be with her?' She bit her lip. 'I'm sorry—I shouldn't have said that. It's not really my business.'

'As it happens, one of the reasons concerns you.'

She had taken Carmen's place on the settee beside him and she now turned to look at him with interest. 'It does? In what way?'

He spoke quickly in a low voice that would not reach the kitchen. 'First, let me tell you the other reason. There are still several details I wished to learn concerning the situation between Carmen and Sloane. She'd been very much in love with him, and I've been endeavouring to discover whether that love is now dead—or whether it's still alive.'

'I see.' She looked at him searchingly. 'Naturally,

you'd think twice about taking her back if you suspected her love for him is still alive.' The quaver in her voice was difficult to control before it betrayed her inner emotion.

'Naturally,' he agreed with a flash of amusement.

'And your other reason? How could it possibly concern me?'

'Surely it's obvious? I feel it's most necessary to keep her away from you. I have no intention of allowing her to continually needle you with hurtful remarks.'

'Are you sure she'd do that?'

'You can bet on it. Her aim would be to make you so hopping mad you'd pack your bag and fling yourself out of the apartment. After that, she'd make Jodie the excuse for settling in.'

'Haven't you forgotten she's afraid of catching measles?'

'Not at all. But by the time you'd left in a rage the worst of the isolation period would be over, and she wouldn't be so afraid to move in. I don't intend that to happen. I know the court gave her access to visit the child, but I shall not allow her to move in.'

Donna sent him a wan smile as she said quietly, 'Thank you for considering my welfare in the battle against Carmen's comments.'

Her spirits rose as she realised he didn't wish to see her upset or hurt by the barbed remarks that could spin off his ex-wife's sharp tongue, and this knowledge filled her with a sense of serene happiness. However, his next words removed much of her satisfaction.

After a pause he continued, still in a low voice, 'I don't think you see the main point. If she moves in here it will help to hasten her divorce from Sloane—and it will give him the reason to end their marriage. Do you imagine I want that to happen?'

'No, I suppose not,' she muttered in a dull voice, realising that the base of his concern had not been on her behalf at all. It had been for himself and the tricky situation in which he'd be placed. Of course—since he was a lawyer—this had been clear to him from the start, so it was no wonder he didn't want her to move out so that Carmen could move in.

As for her own situation, she'd been a fool to have gone along with his charade of love scenes. Her own emotions were now well out of hand and she wondered if she'd ever get over the longing to be held in his arms. Was it only last evening that she'd been so close to him on the bed? The memory made her catch her breath.

'Something's bugging you,' he said quietly. 'Tell me about it.'

She looked at him in dumb misery but, before her mind could find a reply, Carmen came into the living-room with a tray. On it were three glass dishes filled with shrimp cocktail.

'That's for starters,' she declared smugly. 'Really, the dishes in those cupboards bring back such wonderful memories. I just love that Royal Doulton dinner set——'

Next came a French quiche of asparagus and cheese, with the rest of the meal being less exotic, as it consisted of a salad served with boneless rolled chicken, potato chips, tomatoes, beetroot and anything else Carmen could find to go with it.

They were half-way through the meal when Jodie came running into the room, her expression aggressive as she stood beside Donna's chair. *'You go home,'* she said in clear, ringing tones.

Shocked by the attack, Donna could only stare at her in silence.

'What's the meaning of this?' Grant snarled angrily.

Jodie turned to him. 'Tell her to go home,' she demanded belligerently. 'Tell her we don't want her here——'

Grant's eyes narrowed as he surveyed the child. 'Go back to bed at once,' he rasped. 'I'll not tolerate such rudeness.'

Jodie became agitated. 'Mummy said I gotta tell Donna to go home. Mummy said I gotta tell you to—to tell Donna——' She paused uncertainly, trying to remember what Mummy had said, and in desperation turned to Carmen. 'What—what have I gotta say?'

Carmen had the grace to turn pink. 'Nothing, dear— now go back to bed at once like a good girl.'

Jodie's lip quivered. 'But you told me to say——'

Carmen's mouth tightened. 'If you don't leave this room I shall become very annoyed.'

Jodie burst into tears, then fled, shrieking loudly.

Grant glared at Carmen. 'Nice work,' he gritted.

Donna was filled with sympathy for Jodie. She left the table and followed the little girl into her bedroom, but her offers of comfort were met with no response.

'Go away. Go away.' Jodie shouted, then lay sobbing in the bed, her head hidden beneath the blankets.

Donna returned to the table. 'Poor child, I'm afraid she's quite upset. I was unable to console her.'

'She'll get over it,' Grant said gruffly. He turned to Carmen with a satirical glint in his eyes. 'Now that's what I call a clear case of being hoist by one's own petard.'

She became sulky. 'I don't know what you mean.'

'Oh, yes you do. You were caught in your own trap. You should have known better than to have relied upon the child to fire the bullets you made. She's too young.'

'At least she gave Donna the message,' Carmen snapped coldly. Then her attitude changed as she turned to Grant pleadingly. 'My dear, please don't let us quarrel. We've had such a wonderful day and you promised to take me out again tomorrow. Shall we drive to Rotorua? It's so fascinating——'

Grant hesitated, frowning as he thought about it.

'It's only a little over fifty miles away,' Carmen persisted. 'We could go to the thermal area to see the boiling mud pools and geysers. It's years since I last saw that old Pohutu geyser shooting so high in the air. Yes, let's go to Rotorua.' She clasped her hands while her eyes shone at the prospect.

He sent her a hard look. 'Suppose I take Donna out instead? You could spend the day getting to know Jodie. The child would be more delighted than you can imagine.'

Donna's heart leapt at his words. Did he really mean it? She hadn't been to Rotorua which was famous for its thermal activity, and the thought of Grant taking her there filled her with excitement. But it was short-lived, because his attention was again with Carmen, who appeared to cringe at the thought.

'Oh no, not tomorrow,' she protested. 'Perhaps the next day, or the one after that. As soon as those awful spots have gone Jodie and I will become very close. Just you wait and see.'

'A typical fair-weather friend,' he said coldly.

'Grant, dear, can't you remember how these things *affect* me? It's because I'm so—so *fastidious*.'

'Very well.' He turned to Donna and placed a hand over hers as he said quietly, 'Don't worry—your turn will come.'

'It will?' But the smile she sent him did not reach her eyes, which were filled with bleak disbelief.

He sent her a long, steady look. 'I promise you—the day will come when I'll take you to Rotorua.'

Again she forced a smile. 'Just as you'll take me out in the launch? Please, don't let it bother you. I couldn't care less about it,' she lied.

Carmen cut in, speaking eagerly to Grant. 'Tomorrow we'll go to the Rainbow Springs, and to the Fairy Springs. It's years since I've walked along the bush paths to see all those hundreds of trout swimming in their pools.' She turned to Donna with a little laugh. 'You'll be able to think of us standing knee-deep in ferns. It's so *romantic*. Most lovers go there.'

Donna controlled her irritation. She stood up and spoke to Grant. 'I'll wash the dishes while you make plans for tomorrow. When I come back I'll bring the coffee.'

'Thank you,' Carmen cooed sweetly.

But Donna hardly heard the words, because the ache in her heart filled her with misery. You stupid idiot, to allow him to get you into this state, she raged inwardly as she rinsed and stacked the plates into the dishwasher.

She remained in the kitchen until the spasm of self-pity had passed and she felt more composed. Then, carrying the tray bearing the coffee-pot and cups back to the living-room she was surprised to see that Jodie had returned and was again standing beside the table.

'Mummy——' The child's voice was pleading. 'If I wake up tonight will you take me to the loo?'

Carmen frowned, leaning away from her slightly. 'Surely a six-year-old girl can take herself,' she exclaimed.

'Not when I got measles,' Jodie declared stubbornly. 'Donna—she took me last night——'

Carmen appeared to be bored. 'Really? Poor Donna. Had to get out of a nice warm bed, did she?'

Jodie shook her head. 'No, she came out of Daddy's room.'

Carmen drew a deep breath as she stared wordlessly from Grant to Donna.

Grant chuckled. 'Message received?' he asked.

'Well, really——' Carmen flashed a look of hatred towards Donna, then she turned to Jodie. 'I may not be able to help you tonight, dear, but the time is coming when I'll be able to help you *every* night. Isn't that so, Daddy?' She appealed to Grant with a hint of defiance that dared him to deny it in front of the child.

'It's quite possible,' he said to Jodie who looked at him expectantly. 'Now run along to bed *at once*.'

'Goody, goody,' she said, disappearing obediently.

Donna looked at Grant as she sipped her coffee. *It's quite possible*, he'd said, the words thumping in her mind with dull thuds. In one sense they had shocked her, yet in another they'd failed to surprise her. But one thing was certain—they proved he was slowly capitulating to the earlier spell Carmen had cast over him.

By taking Carmen out and away from the apartment each day, he might be saving herself from being needled by his ex-wife's sharp tongue, but he was also placing himself back into square one, where his old infatuation for her was in danger of blossoming once more.

Later, as she lay in her bed, she clenched her fists while she wondered how much longer she could tolerate this situation. Staring wide-eyed through the darkness she recalled that Grant had promised to take her out in the launch. But when would it happen? And more recently he'd said he'd take her to Rotorua. Again—*when*?

He didn't impress her as being a man who broke his promises, yet how could these particular ones to herself be kept while Carmen constantly demanded his attention? Even the idea of it being a case of protection for herself was beginning to wear terribly thin.

Next day she felt more cheerful. There was an improvement in the weather, the dark clouds of yesterday having disappeared beyond the eastern mountain ranges. The strong wind dropped and the lake became dotted with fishing craft of all types and sizes. Aubrey's Place appeared to be busy as people came and went and, watching the activity from the balcony, Donna wished she could go downstairs and help Beryl.

Strangely, she now felt herself to be part of the place, although she suspected that this was because Grant had held her closely and had kissed her lovingly before leaving for Rotorua with Carmen.

She had been in the kitchen wiping the bench when he had taken the cloth from her hand. He had then turned her to face him, his arms enveloping her to press her against the length of his body while his lips had found her own.

For a while the kiss had been gentle, even leaving her mouth to brush other parts of her face, but suddenly his grip on her body had tightened as his hard mouth returned to her lips with a passion that left her breathless. As usual, every pulse had leapt at his touch and she had responded with an ardour she was unable to control.

'Be here when I arrive home,' he'd muttered huskily.

'Of course. What makes you think otherwise?'

'I've been wondering if you're losing faith in me.'

The words puzzled her as she watched him go down the back stairs, and it was only after he had left that she realised the embrace had been unnecessary because Carmen had not been there to observe it. Nevertheless, it made her feel that perhaps he *would* keep his promise to take her out in the launch—or perhaps to Rotorua.

It was late in the afternoon when they returned from Rotorua. Carmen chatted incessantly about the wonders of the thermal area, the beauty of the Rainbow and Fairy Springs, but Donna hardly heard her because she had something else on her mind.

Grant noticed her silence. 'You're all right?' he asked.

'Yes, but I have news for you. The spots on Jodie's face are disappearing. Her forehead is now clear and the ones on her cheeks and chin are fading.' She had been pleased to see the little girl's improvement, although she knew it heralded the end of her stay in Grant's apartment.

'Thank heavens she's on the mend,' Grant said.

'It's marvellous!' Carmen exclaimed. 'When the rest have gone I'll be able to go into her room.'

'You can prepare to make a start on Tuesday,' Grant informed her.

She gaped at him. *Tuesday?* But they won't be all gone by then.'

He went on relentlessly, 'Tomorrow I've said I'll take you to Hamilton to see your parents. Have you even bothered to contact them since you've been back in New Zealand?'

'No. I—I was waiting to see your reaction to my return—so that I'd be able to tell them——'

'Yes? Tell them what?' he cut in.

'That—that I'm *home* again, of course.' Carmen looked at him anxiously, awaiting confirmation of this state of affairs.

'Whatever you imagine you'll be able to tell them, it's time you made contact. After all, they are your parents.'

'So—what are your own plans for Tuesday?' Carmen demanded.

'I'm taking Donna out in the launch,' he told her coolly.

# CHAPTER NINE

GRANT'S words caused Donna to catch her breath. So he *did* intend to keep his promise to take her out in the launch! An inward glow of excitement sent her pulses beating at a faster rate, but outwardly she remained calm as she heard him speak to Carmen in a voice that grated harshly.

'Don't you think she deserves a break?' he demanded.

Carmen shrugged. 'I suppose so,' she admitted reluctantly.

Donna sent Grant a cool stare. 'You don't have to bother, if you consider it to be a chore,' she informed him with a hint of pride.

'It is not a chore,' he assured her sharply.

'Thank you, I'll look forward to it,' she returned quietly.

'I'll bet you will,' Carmen snapped.

Donna felt she could afford to ignore the remark. So—on Tuesday Grant would be taking her out in the launch. She felt exhilarated by the thought, but warned herself it was merely an act of duty—something he felt he had to do to show his gratitude for the days she'd spent in caring for the child. And after all, what more could she expect?

The next day was spent in a haze of happy anticipation of going out on the lake with Grant and, although she repeatedly told herself not to rely upon any magic moments emerging from it, she was unable to shake off her continued state of subdued excitement. Would he hold her close to him? Would he kiss her? Or did he consider that *practise* was now no longer necessary?

Jodie's voice floated from the bedroom to shatter her daydream. Calling petulantly the child said, 'Donna—

150

Donna—I want to get up. I'm sick of staying in bed. When can I get up?'

It was easy to understand the child's impatience and, looking at her reflectively, Donna recalled Doc Fraser's instructions. 'Doctor Fraser said you must stay in bed for a week,' she reminded Jodie. 'But now I do believe that week is up, so this afternoon you may sit on the settee and watch *Sesame Street*.'

'Goody, goody—I love Kermit and Big Bird and all the others——'

'In fact, you may now get up for a short time each morning and afternoon, but you must promise not to go outside or you might catch a chill.'

Jodie nodded vigorously. 'I promise.'

'And tomorrow there's a big surprise for you.'

The child looked at her expectantly. 'Someone will bring me a present?'

'I mean that your mother will be with you all day. Isn't that as good as a present?'

Jodie considered the question seriously, obviously weighing the thought of a present against a day with her mother, until at last she said, 'Yes, I want to be with my mother all the time.'

Later, as Donna wrapped a blanket round the small shoulders to keep Jodie warm while on the settee, she knew that this was yet another step nearer the end of her sojourn in Grant's apartment. However, she brushed the depressing thought aside and told herself to cope with the problem of leaving when that awful day dawned.

But there was nothing awful about the dawning of the next day. Tuesday presented a crisp, frosty morning, the cloudless sky reflected in the deep blue of the lake that lay like an enormous sheet of glass. And as Donna sprang out of bed, instinct told her it would be a day to remember.

She showered, then dressed in her tartan trews and green jersey, and, as she attended to her make-up, the appetising odour of sizzling bacon, eggs and tomatoes wafted from the kitchen. It told her that Grant was there ahead of her, and when she entered the room he looked so handsome in his dark blue trousers and cream polo-neck jersey her heart almost turned over.

'I've attended to Jodie,' he grinned. 'I've plied her with bacon and warned her against greasy fingers being wiped on the sheets.'

'You're so efficient,' she said, looking at the tea and toast already made.

He shrugged. 'Have you forgotten I've been looking after myself for the last three years?'

She forced herself to keep her tone light. 'It's my guess that those lonely days are nearly over.'

'You really believe that?' he asked, his tone suddenly serious.

She nodded, unable to speak.

He put a plate of food on the table then commanded sternly, 'Sit down and eat this. When you've finished, I suggest you get to work on some of those tasty egg sandwiches you're so good at making. We'll also take a thermos filled with soup.'

She was busy making the sandwiches, mashing mayonnaise and chopped parsley into the hard-boiled eggs when Carmen arrived. A quick glance at the white sailor suit that had previously been worn to go out in the launch with Grant filled Donna with suspicion, and as she sensed Carmen's air of determination she became conscious of a sinking feeling.

Carmen glanced at the pile of thinly sliced bread. 'Make enough sandwiches for three,' she ordered brightly. 'I've decided to come with you.'

Donna looked at her blankly. 'But—but what about Jodie?'

'She'll be all right,' Carmen declared casually. 'She's well on the mend now, so I've arranged for Kiri to come up and spend some time with her.'

At that moment Jodie came into the kitchen, hopping with excitement as she smiled happily at her mother. 'Donna said you'll stay with me today.'

Carmen's face became sorrowful. 'Did she, dear? Well, I'm very much afraid she made a mistake. She meant that *Kiri* will stay with you. You like Kiri, don't you? She'll read stories to you——'

The child's face crumpled as tears filled her eyes and she began to weep. 'I don't want Kiri, I want you, Donna said you'll stay with me all day——' The words were punctuated by sobs.

Grant came into the kitchen. 'What the devil's going on? What's the matter with Jodie?'

Carmen said quickly, 'Oh, it's nothing. She's just a little upset because I've arranged for Kiri to come up and spend the day with her—when she's got time, that is——'

He frowned. 'You've *what*?'

'Beryl said she could spare Kiri for a few hours today——'

'*I don't want Kiri,*' Jodie screamed in a fury.

'What *is* all this about?' Grant demanded, his tone exasperated.

'It's simple, dear,' Carmen explained. 'I've decided to come out in the launch with you and Donna. Now, tell me you're *pleased*. But then—I *know* you are.' She clasped his arm and looked up at him appealingly.

Donna held her breath as she waited for Grant's reply. She turned round and leaned against the bench, watching him as he looked down into Carmen's upturned face. Was this perfect day, for which she'd waited so long, about to be snatched from her?

When he spoke it was with surprising gentleness. 'Carmen, you don't appear to be abreast of the situation. Doesn't it occur to you that Jodie is looking forward to having a whole day with her mother? She's really excited about it and I do not intend to allow the child to be disappointed in this manner.' His face had become grave as he stared at Carmen.

'Oh—phooey—children get over disappointments in five minutes,' she retorted airily. 'By tomorrow she'll have forgotten about it.'

'That's possible,' he retorted, then went on bluntly, 'but give her a few years and she'll remember this day. She'll also look back on the fact that her mother *deserted* her for three years—and she will then look at you with a mighty big question in her eyes.'

Carmen sent him a slow smile that broadened as it reflected her delight. 'Grant, dear—do you realise what you're saying?'

'I know exactly what I'm saying.' The words were clipped.

'You're saying that Jodie will have her mother back. It means we'll be *together*—the *three* of us.'

He looked at her in silence, grim lines about his mouth, a scowl clouding his brow.

Donna watched his glum expression with sinking spirits. It seemed to her that he was in the throes of swallowing a bitter pill that would do nothing to cure the situation in which he now found himself.

Carmen went on as though she now had her own situation well in hand. 'Very well, I'll spend the day with Jodie while you take this silly twit of a girl out in your boat. As you said, she's earned a break in the fresh air.' She swept a look of derision over Donna as she led Jodie back to her bedroom.

Donna sighed as she turned back to the sandwiches. A silly twit of a girl, Carmen had called her. How right she was! And as she listened to the excited chatter and laughter coming from Jodie's room, she sighed again as she recalled her own opinion concerning the importance of the family unit. Only now it seemed as if that same opinion had turned into a chicken that had come home to roost, to flap its wings in her face!

Half an hour later they were out on the lake. Grant had

said very little as he'd assisted Donna into the launch and, noticing his silence as the bow cut through the calm waters, she became aware of his depressed mood.

Searching in her mind for a topic that would lift him from it she turned to look back at Aubrey's Place, and as she gazed at the length of building nestling against the brilliant autumn foliage she remarked in a light tone, 'I can understand why you love it. The place has atmosphere.'

He glanced at her quickly. 'You can feel it?' Then, after a pause, 'What sort of atmosphere—would you say?'

She looked at the white timbers shining in the morning sun, the smoke rising from the community lounge chimney, and at the cars parked near the building. 'It's a place where old friends meet,' she decided at last.

He appeared to be pleased by her definition. 'Yes, Aubrey's Place has always been just that. A place where old friends meet. And if you could hear the yarns of the fishermen when they meet in the community room you'd be ready to believe that old Aubrey's still around—somewhere——'

'And you hope to keep him there?'

'He meant a lot to some of those older men.'

'I haven't been in the community room yet—I went upstairs almost as soon as I arrived, you understand—but I presume you have a photo of Aubrey there?'

He frowned. 'No, actually I haven't——'

'Wouldn't it be nice to have him there? It needs a good enlargement, that would put him back among his friends. People like Doc Fraser would love to be able to look at it.'

'You're right. I should have thought of it ages ago.'

'I presume you do have pictures of some sort on the walls?'

'Yes, they're prints of various scenes in the Taupo area. There's one of the Huka falls, the Aratiatia Rapids and the geo-thermal power project. You'll have passed it coming in to Taupo.'

'Oh yes, that place of billowing steam and muted thunder.'

'Carmen chose them all.'

*Carmen.* Was she always on his mind? she wondered bitterly, then, unable to control her irritation she said in a scathing tone, 'In that case they mustn't be removed.'

He did not reply for several moments, appearing to be busy with the handling of the launch. Then, staring across the bow as *Aquarius* rode the smooth water he said nonchalantly, 'Something tells me that you'd change them. To what, may I ask?'

'To photos that apply to the fishing lodge. I see it as a gallery of special interest to the people who frequent the place. There could be photos of excellent catches made by various launch parties, or perhaps of a large trout with the person who caught it—even a group busy at the fish-cleaning trough. You can imagine the sort of photos I mean. They'd become a history of the place.'

He was thoughtfully silent until at last he said, 'Have you anything else in mind?'

A smile touched her lips as enthusiasm began to stir her imagination. 'That view of the lodge from the lake makes a pleasant scene. Why not commission an oil painting of it to be done? It could be hung over the mantelpiece. Aubrey's Place in all its autumn glory. Taupo must have several good artists.'

'It has—and I know a man whose work I admire. I'll talk to him about it.' Unexpectedly his arm shot out and dragged her against his side. His head bent as he brushed her cheek with his lips. 'You seem to be full of good ideas. Have you any others?'

She had, but was unable to voice them as they concerned the relationship between themselves, rather than the fishing lodge. But even if she was to be denied a full cake of happiness she could at least enjoy these few crumbs—therefore she leaned against him, basking in the feel of his arm about her body.

By that time they were far out on the lake in a world of their own. She became aware that the revs of the motor had been reduced to a low murmur, and that the launch was doing little more than drifting lazily while he held her against him. His fingers ran through her hair, holding the back of her head immobile while his mouth sought hers.

It was a searing kiss that sent flames shooting through every nerve, yet her thoughts were clear enough to know that this was madness, and that he had no right to taunt her with desire when he was about to take Carmen to bed.

Yet she was helpless to resist the pleasure that engulfed her as he crushed her against the length of his body, and, realising that his need was as great as her own, her arms tried to hold him even closer. A small shuddering moan of ecstasy escaped her and, while she longed to pour out the depth of her love for him, she managed to control her tongue.

At last, when his lips found their way to her throat she whispered hoarsely, 'This is crazy—utterly crazy—you're forgetting Carmen.' Somehow the last words were wrenched from her.

'That's what you think,' he muttered savagely, yet without releasing her. Instead he found her mouth again and, as the breeze stirred the lake to ripples, it seemed to lift her up towards clouds of rapture. For a while she gave herself up to the dream, delighting in the feel of his hands and then his lips on her breast, but suddenly she came to her senses, finding the strength to push against his chest. 'Grant—are we quite mad? I—I just can't take any more——'

His voice vibrated on a deep note. 'I could make love to you right here on this launch——'

She looked at him in dumb agony, then shook her head as she uttered one word. 'Carmen——'

'Forget Carmen,' he gritted harshly as he stared at her intently, his eyes seeming to bore into her mind as though trying to drag her inmost thoughts and emotions out into the daylight. 'But perhaps you're right. This is madness, and if I don't attend to *Aquarius* heaven alone knows where she'll take us.' His arms left her abruptly and he returned to the wheel.

It was as though he'd suddenly pushed her away from him, and, shocked by the extent of the anticlimax that swamped her, she sank down on to a nearby seat. Intense disappointment caused her eyes to become blurred by tears, and as she brushed them away angrily she searched her mind for a more normal subject. It was the glisten of the water that gave it to her.

'The lake is really quite large,' she remarked at last.

'There are two hundred and thirty-eight square miles of it,' he told her nonchalantly. 'But don't let these calm waters fool you. They can become rough when storms blow up, and there has been more than one boating tragedy on the lake.'

She gazed across the expanse to where other craft dotted the lake, some riding placidly, others speeding along with water skiers behind them. And then a low, rounded mountain rising in isolation to the north-east caught her attention. 'I suppose that huge hump has a name?' she asked, determined to maintain a casual air.

'That's old Tauhara, an extinct volcano,' Grant told her. 'The name means lonely mountain. It rises to three thousand, six hundred feet, so the panoramic view from the top is magnificent. I'll take you up there some day.'

She wondered if she'd heard his last words correctly. 'You will?'

'The return climb takes about three hours. Would you like to do it on a nice clear day?'

She drew a deep breath. 'I'd love to—but aren't you forgetting Carmen? I don't think she'd approve of us being alone—up there.'

'Carmen will have no say in the matter.'

'Oh? She won't?' Puzzled, she waited for further explanation but, as he remained silent, she found herself forced to say, 'From your conversation in the kitchen I gathered that you'd decided to settle down with her—as a family.'

'Don't you think that Jodie should have a family? I seem to remember hearing you hold forth on the matter of family,' he added.

'Of course, I couldn't agree more,' she replied in a dull voice. It would mean joy for the child, but the end for herself. As for the climbing of Tauhara, no doubt they'd do it before she left Aubrey's Place, and before he brought Carmen back into his apartment.

His voice cut into her thoughts as he said, 'The entire district is full of Maori legends. It is said that once upon a time in the dim long ago, this lake was a vast, dry basin. At least, it was until a Maori priest with magic powers climbed Tauhura. He gazed over the wide expanse, muttered a few incantations, pulled up a young tree and flung it down into the dry basin. Then hey presto! The waters gushed forth from where the branches pierced the earth.'

She laughed. 'A likely story. What did he do then? Learn to swim?' Somehow the story had lifted her spirits.

'No. He went further south to kindle the fires of those three volcanoes. No doubt about it—the early Maoris had some mighty men.'

'Obviously it was he who caused Taupo to become a magic place for fishermen,' she smiled, relieved to be feeling happier.

As the launch moved along without too much speed, Grant pointed out places of interest along the shore, and in some strange way the hours flew past more quickly than ever before.

The lunch Donna had prepared was adequate and, as they enjoyed it, Grant looked at her with a twinkle in his eye. 'You make very tasty sandwiches. I've decided to keep you on.'

She knew the words were spoken in jest, yet they failed to amuse her. Nor could she think of a reply that would not betray her emotions, therefore she remained silent.

After lunch, they spent time fishing. Grant caught a trout that pleased him by its size. He showed Donna how to manipulate a rod and she held it patiently until a tug on the end of the line brought forth a shriek of excitement.

He leaned across to raise her rod, driving the hook home, but as the fish leapt from the water he took the rod from her and began to reel rapidly.

'Pass the net,' he ordered.

She did so, then watched as he scooped the fish into the net, unhooked it, then tossed it back into the lake.

She was disappointed. 'That was my first fish—you've thrown it back!' she protested.

'It's too small,' he explained. 'There's a law concerning the size of fish taken from the lake. Carmen would hoot with derision if you took that one home.'

'So what would be different about that?' she queried sharply. 'Carmen hoots with derision over everything that concerns me.'

He didn't bother to deny it. Instead he glanced at his watch. 'It's three-thirty. I'm afraid it's time we were getting back. I'm sorry the day has to be cut short.'

She looked at him with eyes clouded by depression. Was he really sorry? 'I understand,' she said quietly. '*Carmen* will be waiting. You've never really got over her, have you? She's never been very far from your thoughts.' Furious with herself, she felt her eyes grow misty and, turning away, she stared unseeingly across the lake.

'That's what you believe? Let me assure you it's not actually Carmen who is dragging me home. Have you forgotten that this is Tuesday? Didn't you yourself take the message? Isn't someone coming to see me at five o'clock?'

She was startled. 'Oh, yes—you mean the man on the phone. I'd forgotten about him. What makes you so sure he'll come to the lodge?'

'Because I arranged for him to do so.'

She looked at him curiously but asked no further questions. If he wished to confide he would give her a few details, but lawyers did not normally discuss their clients outside the office, and she could only presume that this man was someone with an urgent problem. Or perhaps it was the estate agent, as she'd decided when he'd phoned.

The speed of their return did nothing to help her depression, and they were back in the lodge well before five o'clock. Carmen viewed their early return with pleased surprise.

'Grant, darling—you're home *already*,' she exclaimed with much satisfaction, then went on chattily, 'Jodie and I have had a *marvellous* day. I've been through all her clothes to see what she has to wear, and I've promised her we'll always be together now.'

'It sounds as if you've set the scene for a happy future,' Grant chuckled as though something about this thought amused him.

'Of course I have.' She went on eagerly, 'Do you notice how I've changed the places of some of the furniture in the room? I've pulled the table nearer the glass doors so we can look out on the lake while we're having our meals—and I've moved the settee so that we can sit closer together as we watch television. Can we leave them that way?' she pleaded anxiously.

He shrugged. 'I suppose so—at least in the meantime.' He gave his watch a hasty glance. 'I've left a trout at the cleaning trough. I'll go down and gut it.'

'Tell Roy to do it. He's your servant, isn't he?' Carmen's tone was imperious.

Grant ignored the remark as he hurried towards the back stairs.

Carmen turned to Donna, her attitude of having taken

over the running of the apartment being all too plain. 'He needn't think I'm cooking that trout this evening. I've prepared a cold salad meal so that it didn't matter what time you returned home, but I must say I didn't expect him to bring you back *quite* so early. Got bored, did he?' She sent a smile of quiet triumph towards Donna.

'It's possible,' Donna admitted quietly. 'But it's not the reason we came home early.'

'No? What are you saying?'

'He's expecting a visitor at about five o'clock.'

Carmen was startled. 'A visitor? He didn't tell me.'

Donna smiled. 'No? How strange.'

Carmen glared at her. 'You must know who it is.'

Donna shook her head. 'I've no idea—although I wondered if it could be that estate agent, Bill Adams.'

Carmen began to pace about the room. 'If it is, I won't see him. He needn't think he can bring the fellow here with a list of the flats he's got on hand. No doubt he's being very smart. If he can't get me to the fellow he'll bring the man to me. Grant's a deep one who can be very shrewd in his own way.'

'Well, you can always run away before he gets here,' Donna suggested with a laugh.

Carmen flashed a malicious glance at her. 'Oh yes, I know you'd like to be rid of me, but I'm afraid it won't work. I'll stay and face this estate agent. I'll put him in his place right away. You just watch me——'

Donna was unable to listen to more. She left Carmen to deal mentally with the expected visitor while she herself showered and changed into a cream dress she had not yet worn. It helped to give her confidence which had been sadly lacking. The dress was more feminine that the tartan trews but, although she brushed her hair until it shone and took extra care with her make-up, she still felt inadequate and unable to compete with Carmen's sophistication and her air of possessiveness where Grant was concerned.

She was also frustrated by Grant's easy compliance with Carmen's wishes. He had impressed her as being a strong man, yet, when faced by his ex-wife's demands, he appeared to become a piece of putty in her hands. No wonder he'd asked for help from herself, but for all the good it seemed to be doing he needn't have bothered. And as for the affect his kisses had upon herself—she had only to think of them to feel a flush creep over her body.

The thought of Carmen's presence caused her to linger in her room for as long as possible; however, by five-thirty she feared she was making herself conspicuous by her absence, therefore she returned to the living-room, and here she came upon what appeared to be a cosy family scene.

Grant, who had showered and changed into dark-brown trousers and a light fawn shirt, was pouring drinks, while Carmen sat on the settee beside Jodie. The little girl, who was now looking much better, was having a light evening meal that had been set on a tray and placed on the coffee table before her.

The child dipped a finger of toast into a boiled egg, then smiled happily at Donna as she said, 'My mother says I can have my tea in here tonight—my mother says if I don't look at the spots on my legs they won't be there because I can't see them.' She took a bite of eggy toast and with her mouth full, added, 'My mother says you're going away. When are you going away?'

Donna ignored the question as she took a glass of sherry from Grant. 'Your guest hasn't arrived?' she asked. 'It's well after five o'clock, in fact, almost fifteen minutes to six——'

Carmen laughed. 'Silly girl—he just made him up because he wanted an excuse to come home early.'

'That's not true, Carmen,' Donna assured her. 'I myself took the message from someone who said he'd be here at five o'clock.'

'Then he's probably changed his mind,' Carmen said airily. 'He's probably gone off to sell a flat to somebody else——' Her words were cut short as the phone rang.

Grant strode across the room to pick up the receiver. 'Hello? Oh, thanks, Beryl—just send him upstairs. The hall door is open, so tell him to walk right in.' He replaced the receiver.

The action was followed by silence in the room as they waited for the visitor to arrive, and then Carmen became agitated. 'Grant, who is this man?' she demanded suspiciously.

He grinned at her. 'Just give him time to get up the stairs and you'll see for yourself.'

Her voice rose as she went on, 'I know you're very smart at doing things in a quiet and subtle manner—but if you think you're being clever by asking that estate agent to come and talk to me, you are very much mistaken. I won't listen to a word he has to say—I refuse to live in a flat in Taupo——'

The words died on her lips as a tall man with conspicuous red hair walked into the room. She sprang to her feet, her face turning crimson as she faced him in angry astonishment. 'Oliver! What are *you* doing here?'

He sent her a brief nod but ignored her question as he shook hands with Grant, who introduced him to Donna. His light brown eyes examined her face with interest as he said to Grant, 'Yes, I can see what you mean—there sure is a likeness.'

Donna was puzzled. Had Grant discussed her face with this man? How could he possibly have done so— and when had it happened?

Carmen snapped impatiently, 'Oliver! I asked, what you are doing here?'

He turned to regard her, his eyes full of mockery. 'You're asking what *I'm* doing here?' he drawled. 'That's mighty rich, when the burning question is what are *you* doing here? Aren't you supposed to be at Surfer's

Paradise? Isn't it in the opposite direction?'

She glared at him defiantly. 'I changed my mind. I decided to come and see my daughter instead. I do have access to her, you know.'

'So I understand. But what brought about this sudden decision?'

'You can believe it had plenty to do with that blonde woman who works in your office,' she lashed at him furiously.

'I presume you mean Faye. I told you there was nothing between us. She was merely working late at nights to make extra money for her trousseau. She was married last Saturday. She and her husband will be living in Perth.'

'Oh, I didn't realise——'

'You mean, you wouldn't *listen*.' He swept the subject aside as his eyes became riveted upon Jodie. 'This is your daughter—Jodie?'

'Of course it's Jodie,' Carmen snapped. 'Who else would you expect her to be?'

Oliver stared at the child intently as though examining every feature. At last he said, 'I wouldn't expect her to be anybody else—at least, not with that red hair and familiar little face.'

Again Donna was puzzled. *Familiar?* What did he mean? She had been under the impression that he hadn't seen Jodie before now.

'I've got measles,' Jodie informed him proudly.

'Have you had measles, Mr Sloane?' Donna asked.

'It would be sad to see you catch them at this critical moment,' Grant added, his tone sardonic.

'There's no fear of that.' The reply came with assurance.

Donna was unable to resist a question. 'This isn't the first time you've seen Jodie, Mr Sloane?'

The light brown eyes looked at her with surprise. 'Yes, it is. What makes you think otherwise?'

Donna smiled at him. 'You referred to her face as being familiar. It made me wonder what you meant.'

'Perhaps this will help to explain.' He took his wallet from an inner breast pocket. The colour photo he extracted was postcard size and the red-haired child smiling from it could have been Jodie.

Donna raised startled eyes to his face. 'Who is she?'

'My sister Pamela, when she was about this child's age.'

Grant took the photo from Donna. Staring at it closely he said, 'The likeness is incredible.'

Jodie's voice rose demandingly. *'Let me see—let me see——'*

Grant passed the photo to her. 'There you are, little one. Take a peep at your Aunt Pamela when she was your age.'

Jodie's eyes became round as she gazed at the photo. 'Is she my *aunty*? Where did I get an aunty? She looks like me——'

Carmen snatched the photo from Jodie, then spoke sharply. 'Aunty, indeed—I won't have her listening to this silly talk.' Her voice became stern. 'Jodie, it's time you were in bed. Go to the bathroom *at once*. Clean your teeth, then get into bed and *stay there*.'

There was a howl of protest. 'I don't want to go to bed!'

Grant spoke firmly. 'Bathroom, then bed.'

They watched Jodie leave the room reluctantly, and then Carmen made an attempt to change the subject. Handing the photo to Oliver she said, 'Put that thing away and tell me how you knew I was here.'

'Grant told me,' he informed her coolly. 'He rang me last Friday night and said you'd landed on his mat. We had a long conversation. It'll be like an explosion on his phone bill!'

'But well worth it,' Grant said. He turned to Donna with a mocking glint in his eyes. 'That was when somebody was so sure. I was talking to somebody else——'

She turned away, annoyed to find her cheeks feeling hot. So he hadn't been talking to Carmen, after all. He had been on a long distance call to Sydney. Apparently he'd rung Oliver Sloane and, while telling him that Carmen had arrived a few other details had been straightened between them. This fact seemed to be proved by his next words to Carmen.

'We cleared up several matters to our mutual satisfaction,' he admitted.

'Which means you were discussing me,' she snapped coldly at Grant.

'That's right—and Jodie as well. The date of her supposed premature birth came up for discussion, plus the fact that Doc Fraser had declared her to be a full term baby. I've always known she isn't my child,' he added quietly.

# CHAPTER TEN

CARMEN sat huddled on the settee while the two men looked at her coldly. Oliver was the first to speak. 'Why didn't you tell me you were carrying my child?' he demanded angrily.

A bitter exclamation escaped her as she turned upon him furiously. '*Tell you*, did you say? And where were you, may I ask? I didn't discover I was pregnant until you'd left for overseas.'

Grant cut in, 'It's known as being left holding the baby, old chap. I've experienced it myself——'

Carmen ignored the interruption while she continued to glare at Oliver. 'The mere fact that you'd gone away indicated you no longer wanted me. But I knew that Grant *did* want me—at least, he did *then*—so I took the only course left open to me. I married him as soon as possible.'

'And that's known as stepping into the breach,' Grant grinned, but with little trace of mirth.

'But I did come back,' Oliver reminded Carmen softly.

'Oh, yes—in your own sweet time,' she retorted. 'But in the meantime I had an unborn child to consider, so what would you expect me to do?'

Donna looked at the two men, waiting for one of them to speak, but neither had anything to say. She felt slightly bemused. It was like being in a theatre and watching a play drawing towards its final curtain.

Grant spoke to Oliver, his tone holding the briskness of cross-examination. 'So you definitely admit to Jodie's paternity?'

Oliver regarded him calmly. 'How can I deny it? Apart from Carmen's admission, she's a young Sloane if ever I saw one. Besides, Jodie's likeness to Pamela's photo speaks for itself. If you hadn't told me about her red hair I wouldn't have thought of bringing it with me.'

'So what are your intentions?' Grant's question came lazily.

'I'll take them both home, of course. I presume I can rely on you to attend to whatever legal procedures are necessary as far as Jodie is concerned— —'

Carmen's voice interrupted him coldly. 'What makes you so sure I'll be willing to go back to Australia with you?'

'You have other plans in mind?' Oliver drawled quietly.

'I—I had thought of staying here—in Taupo——' She turned to Grant, her eyes full of appeal in their search for a trace of encouragement from him.

'That'll be nice for you,' Oliver said smoothly. 'You'll be able to attend the wedding when Donna and Grant get married.'

The words almost sent Donna reeling. She opened her mouth to protest, then had the wisdom to shut it again while she tried to deal with the questions spinning round in her mind. What had given Oliver the idea that she and Grant would be married?

Carmen voiced it for her. 'What makes you think they're getting married? They're not even engaged.'

Oliver shrugged then said, 'I only know what Grant told me when we spoke on the phone.'

Carmen swung round to face Grant. 'Is this true? Did you tell him that you and Donna are to be married?'

'If she'll have me,' he replied quietly. 'I must say you've been very slow to get the message. Shall we drink to new beginnings for all of us?' He crossed to the cocktail cabinet and began to pour Scotch for Oliver and himself.

Watching him with reproachful eyes, Carmen said

shakily, 'I'll have a double Scotch on the rocks. I feel the need of it.'

He poured it for her, handing it to her with a cryptic remark. 'It's time you came to your senses, Carmen. Make things up with Oliver while you have the opportunity.'

She glared at him, then carried her own and Oliver's drink to the end of the room.

Grant turned to Donna. 'Do you also feel the need for something stronger than your usual sherry?'

She shook her head. 'No, thank you.' Then, moving to stand beside him while he poured the drink, she glanced towards the end of the room where Oliver and Carmen appeared to have become deeply engrossed in discussing Jodie. Taking the glass from him, she said in a low voice, 'Grant, there's no need for you to worry.'

His dark brows shot up. 'No? What do you mean? What should I be worrying about?' His eyes held an intangible gleam as they rested upon her own.

She went on in a voice meant for his ears only. 'I'm not silly enough to take more than is intended from those words of Oliver's about—about marriage——'

'Oh? What, exactly, are you saying?' The grey eyes now held a hint of amusement.

'I want you to understand that I realise it's all part of your charade—although I didn't expect the *practice* part of it to reach the stage of being a—a virtual declaration of marriage.'

'I see. This means you're turning me down?' The words were spoken lightly and without any sign of regret.

'Of course. No doubt it's a tremendous relief.' Pride dragged the statement from her.

She waited for him to say something that would deny this accusation, but he remained silent. *Fool*, she told herself. What else do you expect? And then she realised it was not possible for him to have said anything further because Oliver was approaching with a question directed towards herself.

'How long do you think it'll be before Jodie is well enough for air travel?' he asked.

Donna looked at him thoughtfully, mentally counting the days until she said, 'Her isolation period finishes at the end of this week, but don't forget she'll still be in a state of convalescence.'

Grant put in a word of advice. 'You'll have to consult Doc Fraser before you arrange your flights. He's down in unit number three. In the meantime you can move into number one with Carmen. You can be my guests until you leave——'

His last words were interrupted by a wail of distress accompanied by loud shouts of 'No—no—no——'

They turned to observe a tearful Jodie standing in the doorway. Clad in pyjamas and clutching Lulu, she ran into the room to face Oliver like an infuriated tiger cub. 'Are you taking my mummy away from this place?' she demanded.

He looked down at her. 'Yes. I'm taking her back to her own home. Did you know it's across the sea, in Australia?'

Jodie shook her head, then buried her face against Lulu's blonde hair as sobs began to shake her small body.

Oliver brought himself down to a lower level by squatting before her. 'Would you like to come with us?'

The sobs ceased as she peered at him across the doll's head. 'Can Lulu come, too? This is Lulu——'

'Of course, and any other dolls you'd like to bring. But there's just one thing——'

She looked at him expectantly, her eyes wide.

'You must get rid of those nasty old measles. You can't fly across the sea in a big jet, with spots on your body.'

Jodie nodded wisely. 'Donna says I gotta keep warm. I'd better go back to bed *at once*.' And, gripping Lulu tightly, she ran from the room.

Grant uttered a small sigh of satisfaction. 'Well, that appears to have been settled nicely. Now, suppose you two girls rustle up something to eat for a couple of hungry men.'

Carmen swept a baleful glance over Donna. 'You appear to be the hostess—at least for the moment—but I'll help you. In any case, I've already prepared my special coleslaw.'

Donna ignored the remark. This was Carmen's way of giving in gracefully, she decided as they went towards the kitchen, but moments later the thought was immediately cancelled by Carmen's next words.

'You needn't be too sure of Grant Armitage yet,' she almost hissed as she took the coleslaw from the fridge.

'No? What do you mean?' Donna had no wish to discuss Grant with Carmen but was curious to know what she had in mind.

'I mean that I haven't yet made up my mind about returning to Sydney with Oliver. If he thinks I'll come running the moment he snaps his fingers—he has another think coming.'

'So what shall you do?'

'I'll settle in here—at Aubrey's. I'll wait to see what happens as far as you and Grant are concerned.'

'You intend to punish Oliver?'

'Why not? He deserves it. He hasn't convinced me there was nothing between himself and that Faye woman with her baby face and big blue eyes. It's a game that two can play.'

Donna found difficulty in concealing her disgust. 'So that's the real reason you came running to Grant. You don't love him—you were merely using him. If Oliver had been really serious about Faye, Aubrey's Place would have been a haven of refuge—somewhere to hide your injured pride, with Jodie being the excuse for landing on the mat.'

'So what?' Carmen's tone was arrogant.

'I can't see that two wrongs make a right.'

Carmen's lip curled. 'I doubt that you can see very much of *anything*. I suspect you've seen very little of life and that you know nothing whatever of men. As for marrying Grant—there's no ring on your finger—no tangible glitter of diamonds to back up his words.' Her voice echoed scornfully.

Nor would there ever be a ring, Donna thought sadly, but as she felt compelled to defend the reason for its non-existence she said, 'When Grant puts a ring on my finger it'll be one we've chosen together. You appear to forget I've been confined to this apartment ever since I arrived.'

'Aren't you really saying he's not rushing into marriage?'

Donna regarded her steadily. 'Can you blame him? He rushed into marriage the first time and made a *ghastly mistake*!'

Carmen opened her mouth to retort, then shut it again.

Donna felt she'd had the last word. She lifted the laden tray and carried it to the living-room where she began placing cutlery on the table. She noticed that Grant and Oliver were chatting amicably. Their glasses had been refilled and they had become engrossed in the subject of fishing.

Considering the circumstances, the rest of the evening passed surprisingly well, but this was because it was dominated by the two men who continued to talk while Donna and Carmen sat and listened. Nor was it late when Oliver finally stood up and indicated to Carmen that it was time they went downstairs to the unit she was occupying. By that time, Grant had promised him full use of the launch while they were waiting for Jodie to become well enough for air travel.

'That's jolly decent of you,' Oliver said with appreciation.

Grant added, 'If you become bored with fishing, you can always take a run to the Château Tongariro. Carmen thinks it would make an excellent place for a second honeymoon.'

Oliver raised an eyebrow. 'Have you decided to use it yourself for the same purpose?'

Grant shook his head. 'No. When living in this area we're so close to the Château it loses its novelty. I had something much further away in mind—like an overseas trip to Fiji or Norfolk Island where one can bask in the warmth of tropical sunshine.'

Donna's heart gave a lurch as she heard the words and, turning slowly, she regarded Grant with an unspoken question in her eyes. Was it necessary for him to carry the deceit of their bogus engagement to this extent?

The look he sent back to her was long and steady enough for her to sense the sincerity in it and, startled, she wondered if she'd just made a ghastly mistake. Was it possible that his statement to Oliver had not been part of his charade? Surely he couldn't have *meant* that he intended to marry her?

Carmen's words then came back to her. He works in a quiet and subtle way, she'd said. But no—she was now allowing her imagination to be stirred by a bout of wishful thinking, Donna told herself. For pity's sake—he hadn't even said he loved her!

Perhaps it was her intense longing to hear those words that caused her mind to clear sufficiently to realise it was too soon for such definite commitments; and although she felt as if she'd been at Aubrey's Place for almost a lifetime—and as if she'd known Grant for *years*—it was, in fact, little more than a week. Of course—he was giving her *time*. And if this was so, all she had to do was to have patience and wait. And then her ponderings were broken into by Oliver's voice speaking to Grant.

'There's the matter of Jodie's birth certificate,' he said. 'I suppose I should take it with me if you'd be good enough to dig it up.'

'Certainly. It's in the office,' Grant informed him. 'I'll

collect it as we drive through Taupo tomorrow. I intend taking Donna to Rotorua for the day, so you and Carmen can spend the time with Jodie. It'll be an opportunity for you to get to know your daughter,' he finished with a grin.

'The sooner the better, I suppose,' Oliver agreed. 'I haven't yet latched on to the idea of having a daughter.'

'I can assure you it won't take long, old chap,' Grant returned easily. 'All you have to do is wait until little Madam has one of her tantrums.'

'You're forgetting I'm used to dealing with tantrums,' Oliver replied sardonically. He took the glass Grant had refilled and carried it to where Carmen stood watching the lights of cars racing along the highway.

Grant turned to Donna, a hint of amusement crossing his face. 'Do I detect surprise in your eyes?'

She looked at him wonderingly. 'It's possible. You're full of surprises. I didn't know we were going to Rotorua tomorrow.'

'I promised to take you there, didn't I?'

'Yes, but you don't have to bother about it if you've other things to do.'

'Other things—like what?'

'Well, like going out in the launch——'

He was watching her intently. 'Are you saying you don't want to come to Rotorua with me?'

'Oh no, of course not. I'd love to go.' Happy anticipation began to bubble within her. Perhaps tomorrow would be the day when he'd tell her he loved her.

The feeling of hope was still with her when Donna woke next morning, and as she sprang out of bed she saw that the fine weather was still lasting, although to the south beyond the mountains there was a bank of dark clouds.

Mid-morning saw them driving along the lakeside highway towards Taupo township and, as Donna sat comfortably in the seat beside Grant, she tried to still her inner excitement. Calm yourself, stupid, she warned mentally, but, although she made an effort to look upon the outing with casual indifference, her happiness was made evident by her flushed cheeks and sparkling eyes.

Grant sent several glances towards her but did not break the companionable silence between them until he said, 'Are you aware that you look quite lovely this morning? It must be because you feel suddenly free— perhaps like a person who has just come out of prison.'

She nodded, still glowing from his compliment. 'Yes— I suppose I have been somewhat cooped up——'

'I wanted you to know that I appreciate all you've done for young Jodie. I'm truly grateful.'

She bit her lip as she turned away to gaze across the lake. It was neither his appreciation nor his gratitude that she needed.

When they reached Taupo, Grant turned along a side street, then stopped the car before a modern building. 'This is it,' he said.

She looked at the polished brass plate which proclaimed the offices of Armitage and Armitage, Barristers and Solicitors, then was unable to resist a question. 'You own this building?'

'Yes. Dad and I own it jointly.'

'I haven't met your father.'

'No—but that's not surprising. You've had very little opportunity to meet anybody. Would you like to see where I spend my days of toil?'

'Oh yes, please——'

He unlocked the front door and led her inside the building to where panelled walls seemed to indicate a sombre atmosphere. They went beyond the thickly carpeted reception area and along a passage past several doors until he ushered her into an office which was dominated by a large desk. Heavy law books lined one wall, while another wall held shelves filled with neatly folded documents, each one tied with pink tape. Looking at them, she guessed that each bundle represented a client.

Grant went to a filing cabinet that had a large bottom drawer marked Personal. The paper he took from it was placed in his wallet and he then said, 'Before we leave I'll show you the rest of the offices—that's if you'd be interested——'

'Of course I'd be interested, but first I'd like to see you sitting at your desk.'

His dark brows shot up. 'That's a strange request. What's behind it?'

'Just a desire to see you at your work.'

'You're joking, of course?'

'Not really.' She had kept to a bantering tone but beneath it she was in earnest. It would be something further to remember about him when she returned to Auckland.

'Very well, I shall humour your whim.' He unlocked a cupboard and drew forth a wig and black gown. Donning them, he said in a brisk hard tone, 'Now then, Miss Dalrymple, please take the witness stand, or otherwise sit in that chair.'

She sank into the chair and gazed across the desk at him. Was this Grant whose eyes had turned the colour of cold steel? And was there a strange purpose behind his suddenly grim manner?

He continued in a hard accusing voice that echoed round the office. 'You have stated that you are on holiday, Miss Dalrymple.'

'Yes, that's right—at least I'm supposed to be——' she smiled, playing along with his game of portraying himself at work.

'Kindly answer the questions with yes or no,' he snapped. 'You left your lover in Auckland and came to Taupo——'

'*Lover?* I did not,' she denied indignantly.

'What do you mean by saying you did not? You *did* come to Taupo and while there you found yourself in the arms of another man. Yes or no?' His eyes had narrowed to watchfulness.

'Yes—I mean no—but I told you *before*——'

What *do* you mean, Miss Dalrymple?'

She began to feel agitated. 'I mean you've got it all wrong. You know jolly well how I came to be in the arms of another man.'

'Ah—so you admit to there being someone in Auckland?'

'No, I do *not*. You're quite mistaken.' She was dismayed.

'I think not. When this man in Taupo kissed you, your thoughts flew to the lover you'd left behind in Auckland—and so you closed your eyes and responded as though you were with him.'

'*I did not!*' she almost shouted at him, then quailed beneath this glare because suddenly it became apparent that he believed what he was saying. Also, this silly make-believe cross-examination was getting out of hand. It was switching from a game to a serious probing that was not even remotely amusing.

His next words came in a quieter tone. 'I presume you do have men friends in Auckland, Miss Dalrymple?'

'Of course I have men friends, but there's nobody *special*. Do you imagine I'm never taken out dancing or to a movie?' At least she'd got that point across—but did he believe her? Probably not. Frustrated, she felt her eyes grow misty, and before tears could form she said, 'I'm glad I don't have to really face you in court.'

His voice came softly. 'OK, but at least you've seen me in court regalia of wig and gown. Now shall we go to Rotorua?'

She watched as he shrugged off the loose black garment, then removed the small curled headpiece and replaced them in the cupboard. He could have kissed me in here, she thought, her mind filled with sadness, but obviously he had no intention of doing so.

Playing for time, she said, 'I haven't yet seen you sitting at your desk.'

'And so you shall,' he replied with mock severity. Seating himself in the chair he drew out his cheque book and wrote rapidly. Then, handing her the slip of paper he said, 'This is owing to you.'

The action was so unexpected she was taken by surprise and, when her eyes took in the amount on the cheque, she could only give a faint gasp as she said, 'This is utterly ridiculous!'

'You've more than earned it,' he said. 'Actually, it covers two jobs—one concerning Jodie—and, of course, there was myself——'

She met his gaze squarely. 'What I did for Jodie was completely voluntary and to help Beryl. I don't expect to be paid for it.' Her chin rose as she stared at him coldly. 'Nor did I expect to be offered money for accepting the phoney kisses you saw fit to bestow upon me—kisses that had no real meaning at all——'

She stopped abruptly, fearing that her disappointment might cause her to betray the fact that her own response had been anything but phoney. A swift movement tore the cheque in half and, as she tossed it back at him, she added, 'Now, shall we go to Rotorua—or would you prefer to return home?'

'We'll go to Rotorua, because I wish to make a purchase.' He closed his cheque book and left the desk.

She forced herself to smile. 'A present for Jodie, no doubt?'

'Not exactly,' he returned, then added gravely, 'I seem to have really upset you.'

'That's an understatement. You were so adamant that I have an Auckland lover awaiting my return—and what's more, I think you really believe it.'

'But you haven't?' he persisted.

'Of course not.' Her voice rose angrily. 'And you did your best to bully me into admitting something that isn't true.'

'I didn't mean to rile you to this extent.'

'I'll get over it,' she replied calmly. It wasn't the only emotional state she'd have to get over, she realised as they went along the passage towards the front entrance.

As they drew near to the door she paused to examine the indoor pot plants that took away the bareness from the reception area. It was really an effort to give him a last opportunity to take her in his arms, but nothing happened. Minutes later they were speeding along the highway towards Rotorua.

For several miles Donna sat in a state of deep depression until common sense told her to snap out of it before Grant detected her despondency. Nor did this prove to be difficult because he chatted most of the way, directing her attention to points of interest until at last he said, 'Wind down your window and tell me what you can smell. It comes from those puffs of steam rising from the side of the road.'

She obeyed, taking in a deep breath. 'Is it sulphur?'

'Yes. It's Rotorua's own distinctive odour from the thermal activity that's to be found over a wide area. People who live here are so accustomed to it they hardly know it's there.'

'I don't find it unpleasant.'

'Good. You'll get a full share of it when we walk round the geysers and mud pools. But first we'll have lunch.'

They drove into the town, where he took her to a restaurant and, as they ate the well-served meal, she told herself she was being a fool to allow the incident in the office to ruin this day which must be enjoyed to its fullest extent. She also knew he was regarding her intently, and that she'd be an even greater fool to present him with a continually glum face, therefore she forced a smile on to her face.

His grey eyes seemed to probe her mind as he said quietly, 'That's better. You're beginning to feel more as you did when we first set out this morning.'

'You're saying you know how I felt when we left home?' The last word had just slipped out.

'Your face was radiant. It spoke for itself.' He paused for several moments then added, 'You're beginning to think of the lodge as home?'

*Home*. Yes, she had been thinking of Aubrey's Place as home but, as this was not something to be admitted, she thought carefully before she said, 'By the time I leave it will have been home for three weeks because, when Jodie's isolation period is finished, I'll spend the rest of my vacation with Beryl.'

'With *Beryl*?' he echoed, betraying his surprise. 'I suppose that means you'll move downstairs?'

'That's right. I'll go just as soon as Jodie's condition sets me free, although first I'll check with Doc Fraser.'

'Somehow, I've become accustomed to your presence.'

'Really?' She smiled whimsically. 'You're forgetting it was Beryl I came to visit in the first place, but so far I've hardly set eyes on her.'

'And after that?'

'Back to the job, I suppose—answering the phone, making appointments, attending to accounts and doing all that's expected of a doctor's receptionist.'

'Why didn't you fly south to spend the period with your parents?'

'Because they had arranged to go to Australia for the Sydney Easter Show.'

Unexpectedly he said, 'Something tells me that I really upset you in the office.'

She looked at him steadily as she admitted, 'More than you realise. Why did you do it?'

'Because I have to make sure——' He broke off as a waiter approached the table. A bill for the meal was left discreetly on the table. Grant glanced at it, then stood up.

'Let's go to the geyser valley,' he said.

She followed him from the restaurant, inwardly fuming that the waiter should have come at that moment. What had Grant been about to say? That he had to be sure—*of what*? She longed to pursue the subject, but fear of a rebuff kept her silent.

For a short time he drove her along the shore of Lake Rotorua and told her about the strange sights to be seen in the tourist city. He pointed out places where subterranean boiling water sent steam shooting through holes in the ground and where mud bubbled.

'It's a weird place,' she said. 'Didn't Carmen say something about a special geyser?'

'She was referring to old Pohutu. It's at Whaka in the geyser valley. I'll take you there now.'

He drove to the edge of the city, where a parking area was bordered by souvenir shops. They crossed a bridge spanning a river where Maori children dived down into the warm water, searching for coins thrown by tourists. A cluster of small Maori dwellings was passed, and a short distance further on they came to a place where Grant indicated a wide flat terrace. Notices warned the public of danger.

'That's where old Pohutu blows his top,' he informed Donna. 'He gathers force down below and comes up periodically.'

Even as he spoke, a few nearby tourists began to move back as a rush of boiling water emerged from a large hole in the terrace. It gathered momentum until a scalding jet of steam and water spurted skyward in a plume-like fountain that reached to a hundred feet. Fascinated, they watched it play until its activity was spent and it sank back into its hole.

Grant then led her along paths that wound between pools of bubbling water, patches of mud plopping like porridge on the boil, and sulphur-ringed holes that belched steam from deep underground cauldrons of simmering water.

They were walking along a brush-sheltered path when she remarked, 'It's a strange and eerie place. It makes me feel quite nervous. I can't help wondering if ghastly accidents have occurred like—like people falling into boiling pools.'

He nodded. 'I'm afraid the odd accident has been known to happen, although fortunately not very often. But there's no need for you to worry—I love you too much to allow you to go near any places of danger.'

His statement had come so casually that Donna thought she must have imagined the words. Her jaw sagged slightly and her eyes widened as she turned to stare at him. 'What—what did you say?'

He stood still, facing her. 'Didn't you hear me? I said I love you too much to allow you to fall into danger.'

'That's what I thought you said.' She looked at him wonderingly. 'Do you really mean——?' Shyness prevented her from finishing the question.

'That I love you? Of course I do. Surely you *know*?'

'How could I possibly know? You didn't tell me.'

'Hasn't it been obvious?'

She shook her head. 'I thought it was still pretend—that it was part of your make-believe. Practice, you called it.'

'I'm afraid that from an early stage make-believe turned into reality. Almost at once I found difficulty in keeping my hands to myself. I continually wanted to touch you—to hold you close——'

'Don't you know that a girl has to be told these things? She doesn't take them for granted.'

He took both her hands, gripping them tightly. 'Then let me tell you now. My darling, I love you very much. Is it possible that you——?' His voice had become husky.

She nodded, her eyes shining. 'Yes—yes, Grant. I do love you very much——'

He snatched her to him, his lips finding hers in a kiss that betrayed the depth of his longing. Time stood still for as long as it lasted and, although they knew that tourists could come along the path at any moment, it didn't seem to matter.

At last he spoke seriously. 'You'll marry me, my dearest?'

She nodded happily, 'Yes—yes, of course!'

'I must admit I was rocked when you turned me down last night.'

A shaky laugh escaped her. 'How could I turn you down when I hadn't even been *asked*? Oh, yes—I know you told Oliver we're to be married, but it was the first I'd heard of it.'

He gripped her shoulders as he stared down into her face. 'I can only say that it was all very clearly set in my own mind—so firmly, in fact, that I imagined it was also set in your mind. I felt positive you loved me. It seemed to be something that we both knew—something for which no words were necesssary.'

'Yet you told Oliver.'

'Yes. When I phoned him and suggested he should come and collect his wife I also told him I'd found the girl I intended to marry. And that reminds me—I have a purchase to make.'

They returned to the car, then drove back to the city where he was able to park near a jeweller's shop. 'You're about to choose your engagement ring,' he told her.

She was startled. 'This is the purchase you mentioned when we were in your office?'

'That's right. Now you know why I had to be sure there was nobody else. Shall we go into the shop?'

She followed him as though in a dream but, when faced by the velvet-covered trays of diamond rings, she found herself in a dazed state that almost threw her off balance. Everything had happened so quickly, and perhaps it was the unexpectedness of it all that made it impossible to do more than stare at the dazzling display of clusters, bars and solitaires.

At last she picked up one of the latter. It was a modest ring of its type, because the prices shocked her, but she had always preferred a single diamond. In some intangible way it seemed to indicate a oneness between a man and a woman, and that was what she wanted with Grant—to be one with him.

Watching her, he said, 'Shall I tell you which one I'd like you to choose?'

She looked at him gratefully. 'Oh, yes—please—they're all so beautiful.'

Without hesitatation he picked up a much larger solitaire, one that almost took her breath away. Then, taking her left hand, he slipped it on the third finger. It fitted perfectly.

They arrived home to be met by a scene of contented domesticity. Oliver reclined in an easy chair with a pile of fishing magazines on his lap, while Carmen and Jodie sat at the table, a new and larger jigsaw puzzle before them.

The little girl was brimming with importance. 'I've got two fathers now,' she told Donna. 'I've got Daddy Oliver and Daddy Grant. I don't know anybody else with two fathers——'

'That's lovely for you,' Donna smiled. Shyly, she kept her left hand hidden in the pocket of her jacket. There'd be time enough for them to see the flash of her ring.

Jodie beamed at her. 'Doctor Fraser came to see me today. He said I can fly in a plane next week. I'm going with my *mother*.'

Carmen said, 'Personally, I can't get home quickly enough. Oliver has been so sweet and understanding. He's explained everything. I'm afraid I was rather foolish to distrust him and to run away. I'll never do it again.'

Oliver spoke frankly. 'But at least it has brought the

*three* of us together—and it also made me realise how very much you mean to me.' He smiled at Carmen. 'So you see, my dear, most things happen for the best.'

Jodie broke in excitedly. 'Daddy Oliver says I can have a puppy for my very own. He says it'll be a Corgi!'

'There's so much to do,' Carmen exclaimed. 'I intend to redecorate the room Jodie will use—I'll have it done in a child's wallpaper—and I want to buy really pretty clothes for her.'

Donna looked at her wonderingly. Was this the same Carmen who had arrived less than a week ago? No, this was an entirely different woman. That other Carmen had been an unhappy person, frustrated and unsure about what she wanted, whereas this new Carmen appeared to be in a more contented frame of mind. It was almost as if she seemed to be ready and anxious to settle down to motherhood.

Nor was the change in her attitude lost upon Grant. He listened to her plans for Jodie's schooling—only the best would be good enough—and then he extracted the child's birth certificate from his wallet. Handing it to Oliver he said, 'I'll miss the little one. I don't want her to go out of my life completely.'

'There's no need for her to do so,' Oliver assured him. 'Carmen and I have been discussing it, and if it's OK with you she can be flown across the Tasman for the odd school holiday.'

'Sure—we'd love to have her, wouldn't we, darling?' Grant turned to Donna and put his arm about her shoulders.

She nodded, revelling in the sound of his endearment. 'Perhaps she could come back for the summer holidays?'

Carmen's eyes held a question. 'You'll still be here then?'

Donna nodded, then removed her hand from her pocket.

There was a sharp intake of breath, followed by a long

silence, as Carmen stared at the glittering solitaire.
'When are you to be married?' she asked at last.

'As soon as possible,' Grant declared in a determined
tone. 'Impatience is my second name at the moment. I
can't wait to make Donna my wife.'

Donna's eyes shone as her face betrayed her happiness. 'I must give my employer notice and see him settled
with a new receptionist,' she warned, thrilled by his
eagerness. 'It shouldn't take long because the girl who is
filling in for me will probably stay on in my place.'

'And then you'll be married in Dunedin?' Carmen
presumed. She had crossed the room to seat herself upon
Oliver's knee, her arm going affectionately about his
neck.

Donna shook her head. 'No, I'd prefer my parents to
come to Taupo. I don't want a large wedding—just a few
friends at a church in Taupo, and then a reception
at——' She paused to look hopefully at Grant.

'A reception at Aubrey's Place,' he added. Then,
despite the presence of the others, he took her in his arms
and kissed her lovingly.

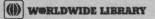

**Deep in the heart of Africa lay mankind's most awesome secret. Could they find Eden . . . and the grave of Eve?**

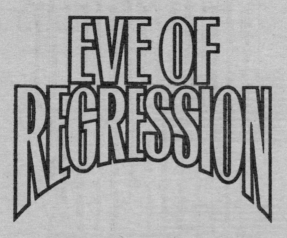

# JOHN ARTHUR LONG

A spellbinding novel that combines a fascinating premise with all the ingredients of an edge-of-the-seat read: passion, adventure, suspense and danger.

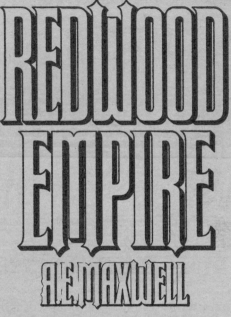
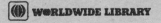